On A Silent Night

S.L. STERLING

On A Silent Night

Copyright © 2018 by S.L. Sterling

All rights reserved. Without limiting the rights under copyright reserved about, no part of this publication may be reproduced, stored in, or introduced into a retrieval system, or transmitted in any form or by any means (mechanical, electronic, photocopying, recording, or otherwise) without the prior written permission of both the copyright owner and the above publisher of the book. This is a work of fiction. Any references to historical events, real people, or real places are used fictitiously. Other names, characters, places, and events are products of the author's imagination, and any resemblance to actual events or places or persons, living or dead, is entirely coincidental. Disclaimer: This book contains mature content not suitable for those under the age of 18. It involves strong language and sexual situations. All parties portrayed in sexual situations are consenting adults over the age of 18.

ISBN
978-1-989566-50-3
978-1-989566-51-0

Editor: Sandy Ebel of Personal Touch Editing

Cover Design: Thunderstruck Cover Design

Dedication

To those who have loved and lost and found love again.

Prologue

Cass - 2015

I got up out of bed and looked out my bedroom window, the dark grey skies that hung overhead threatening another winter storm. It had snowed overnight again, and from the looks of it from the second-story window, it looked like it would be more than my shovel and my back would be able to handle. I watched two young kids across the street in the middle of a full-blown snowball fight, laughing away. I kept watch on them, laughing to myself until I heard a deep moan from the bed.

I turned and glanced at the clock beside my bed—only seven, Brody was still sound asleep but dreaming. I grabbed my bathrobe from the end of the bed, wrapped it around my body, and went downstairs. The floor was cold on my bare feet. I could feel the chill in the air of the house—if it was going to storm today it was only going to get colder. The old house was drafty as it was, needing a lot of work, work I just couldn't afford to do to keep it up. On my way to the kitchen, I stopped and checked the thermostat in the hall—sixty-nine. I turned it up two degrees, wrapped my thin robe tighter around myself, and went into the kitchen.

I turned the coffee maker on, always preparing it before I went to bed the night before, a habit I had gotten in when I first married. I headed straight to my laptop while waiting for it to brew. I sat at the kitchen table, a lot of work to do if I was going to meet the deadline I had set with my editor for the end of the month. Truthfully, I was nowhere even close to making it and was considering asking for an extension. My book sales had fallen, and they were suffering. My publisher really wanted me to continue with the series I had started before Jackson had passed away, and even though I was trying, nothing seemed to be coming to me. I was so beyond stressed. I had only released two books this year, a far cry from my usual, and I was now finding it a struggle to find my voice.

Everything seemed to be very complicated lately—writing, the house, my relationship with Brody—everything! With Brody, trouble hadn't started right away, maybe about a year after Jackson passed. There was no denying it, we were both physically and mentally attracted to one another and had been for a long time. We had flirted back and forth over the past year, dancing around one another like children at a playground. I remembered the first time our eyes had really met, every single touch we shared, and how they would send shock waves through my body. That catch of bare skin, the way his hold on me changed while we cuddled and watched TV, and how one day his touch started to feel more like fire than comfort. I let go of the breath I was holding, got up and grabbed a mug from the cupboard, setting it on the counter.

Last night had happened—it had really happened.

We had been laying together cuddling, watching TV. I had fallen asleep curled into his side. He was like a blanket, always making me feel safe and secure. I felt him slip out from underneath me and opened my eyes in time to see him step away from the couch.

"Where are you going?" I asked, my voice deeply sleep filled. He stopped and turned, tilting his head to look at me.

"Sweetie, it's late." He pulled the blanket up around my shoulders, tucking me in. "I'm going to head home, you need to get some rest."

"Stay with me?" I begged as I inched my ways toward

the back of the couch, making room for him to lie down with me. "Please Brody."

I had been having a bad bout of nightmares lately and really didn't want to be alone. I stared up at him, my eyes pleading. As he looked down on me, I could tell from the look in his eyes he really didn't want to leave me, but something was making him hesitate. He stood there, his eyes running over me.

"Stay, just until I fall back asleep." He pulled the blankets back and sat back down on the couch. He relaxed back and pulled me into him. I rested my head on his strong shoulder and lay my hand across his chest. Within minutes my right leg rested over his, and I had fully relaxed against him, listening to his beating heart.

I inhaled deeply, taking in the scent of him mixed with his cologne and buried my face into his neck. He felt like home, a place lately so unfamiliar to me. I placed a soft kiss on his jawline and whispered, "Thank you," into his ear.

He didn't say anything, turning to look at me. Our eyes finally meeting, he leaned in and grazed my lips. At first, I pulled back—it felt awkward kissing my dead husbands' best friend. I stared into his blue eyes, neither of us saying a word. Without notice, his lips crashed into mine, his hand on my hip, he rolled onto his side, pulling me tighter into him as his tongue forced my lips apart. He pulled me tighter against him yet, his hand on my ass, so this time, I could feel his excitement dig into me. Within minutes, I found myself straddling his waist, grinding down on him. He placed his hands under my ass, picked me up, and carried me upstairs to my bedroom, my legs wrapped tightly around his waist. At first, things were awkward between us, but as we slowly peeled away the clothes from our bodies, both of us became filled with want and need, neither of us denying what we felt for one another.

Sitting here now, thinking back to last night, I could still feel his every kiss and touch. I could still feel him firmly buried inside of me, every deep, forceful thrust that had brought me to orgasm more than once. It had been almost too intense for both of us during some moments.

I jumped when I heard the stairs creak, and I shook myself out of the memory. I poured a cup of coffee, sat back down at the kitchen table, and started checking my email in time to hear a sleepy voice behind me, "Morning." He kissed the top of my head, rubbing my shoulder with his strong hand, and made his way over to the coffee maker, grabbing a mug from the cupboard.

I didn't know what to say, I didn't know how to act, everything felt different to me. His touch even felt different. I could feel fear building inside of me, the fear that things would change so much between us, and our friendship would be over. Instead of saying anything, I sat there quietly, smiled at him, and went back to checking my email, trying to pretend all that happened between us last night wasn't eating me alive.

He stood there, taking me in, sipping hot coffee, not saying much either. And by the time he left that morning, we'd had our first real fight, and everything was more of a mess between us than it ever had been before.

Chapter One

Most of the shops were already closed as I drove down Main Street. I had just transferred and was starting work this week with the Coldhaven Fire Department. After dropping the bags I had at the fire station, I decided to start my way back to Greyfield.

I wanted to see Cass, I had a lot of explaining to do—if she would even let me in the house. Frankly, I wouldn't blame her if she didn't, three years was a long time. I hadn't planned to be gone that long, but the damage had been done. I sent several messages to her over the years via text, primarily because I had been too afraid to call, but they had gone unanswered. I couldn't blame her, I probably wouldn't have answered either if I were her. I wasn't sure if she even had the same cell phone number, but if she did, she was totally ignoring me. Either way, it didn't matter because, in a few hours, I would be face to face with her to say what needed to be said.

Tapping my fingers on the steering wheel, I knew no matter what happened, if she took me back or didn't, I would deserve whatever I got, but my feelings would, at least, be laid out.

I parked my car in front of the little coffee shop that sat on the corner and headed inside. I needed food and a coffee to help keep me awake, it had been a long day of traveling, and it wasn't over yet. As I approached the door, a flyer in the window caught my attention. First Annual Christmas Book Drive & Bake sale at Coldhaven Books, Proceeds to go to Coldhaven's Fallen Firefighters Charity. The Fallen Firefighters charity was near and dear to my heart.

I looked over my shoulder at the darkened storefront of Coldhaven Books. The store must be new, I didn't recall it being here the last time I had driven through, but that had been a few years ago now. The Christmas tree in the window was lit, but the front display barely looked finished. The other stores on the street were just starting their displays as well, some windows completely empty. I opened the door to the coffee shop and walked inside, the few customers who sat eating turning to look my way. I stepped up to the counter and ordered a large black coffee and a bagel to go. While the girl was preparing my order, I looked at the same flyer that sat on the counter.

"Can you tell me a little more about this?" I asked pointing to the flyer.

The girl turned and smiled at me, "Were you wanting to sign up?"

"What do you mean? Sign up?"

"To help out, they are looking for volunteers."

I needed to get some volunteer hours in, anyway, so this was perfect. I nodded in her direction. "Do I need to stop over at the bookstore?"

"No, no, I'm helping out the owner, I have a sign-up sheet. I'm not a hundred percent sure what she will need, but she told me to tell people she would be in touch. All I know is she needs help." She grabbed a form from behind the counter, handing me a pen.

I scribbled my name down on the sheet.

"Yeah, the owner, she lost her husband a few years back now, he was a firefighter. This is the first fundraising event she's done. Sadly, there haven't been too many people interested in volunteering."

I knew the feeling of loss all too well. "Well, I'll pass around the word to the guys at the station. Surely, some of them will want to help out."

"Oh, are you a firefighter?"

I nodded taking my coffee from the other girl who worked behind the counter. "Yep, just transferred here."

"Well welcome to Coldhaven. I'll pass the message to Cassandra," she winked at me.

I near stopped dead in my tracks, my heartbeat accelerating. It had to be a coincidence. "Cassandra?" I swallowed hard.

"Yeah, the owner of the bookstore," she smiled and went back to cleaning out the display cooler, getting ready to place fresh product inside.

I took a deep breath, then started laughing to myself. I needed to calm myself down. After all, it couldn't have been my Cass, she was an author not a bookstore owner.

"Great, thanks. Have a good night." I walked out the front door, the cold air slamming into my face. The air felt like it could snow, and I still had a couple hours drive ahead of me. I climbed into my truck and started it up, music blaring as I pulled away from the curb, heading toward the highway, toward the girl I hadn't, wouldn't, and couldn't forget.

Chapter Two

Cass

Jingle Bells was playing over the radio speakers while I was busy putting the finishing touches on the Christmas display, keeping an eye as people walked by the front of the store. It was close to five, and the streets of downtown Coldhaven were still bustling with shoppers. It was almost closing time. I smiled as I placed the last Christmas book I was going to display in the window under the artificial tree. Maybe this Christmas would be different. I felt I was in a pretty good place. I turned my attention to one of my favorite customers, Cathy who needed to pay for her purchase.

"What do you have today Cathy?" I asked as I went behind the counter.

"Just a couple books for the girls," she smiled at me. Cathy was a widow of one of the men who had passed away fighting that fire last summer, leaving behind Cathy to raise their two baby girls.

"How are the girls?" I asked.

"They're doing okay, this time of year is hard on them."

I nodded in understanding, I knew all too well how hard this time of year was. I grabbed two Christmas bookmarks from behind the counter and threw one into each of the books. "For the girls," I smiled.

"Thank you. Oh, and Cass, I wanted to donate a few trays of baked goods for the fundraiser."

"Great, Cathy! I can send you details if you like."

"Sounds perfect."

I slid the two books into a bag. "Here you go and thank you." I handed her the bag, and she smiled as she took it from me and walked out the door. Just as the door shut, I heard Ray's deep voice come from the back.

"Cass, sweetie, I got a box from the back door." Ray came walking through the curtain that separated the store from the employee area, carrying a box marked *donation*.

"Great! Those are probably for the book drive." I giggled with excitement. He placed the box on the counter, and I started sifting through it. "There are some awesome titles in here. Oh look, the series May has wanted is here. I'll have to call her tomorrow. Could you put it down on the floor?" I asked, pointing to a spot behind the register.

"Sure thing! You sure are happy this afternoon," Ray said, dropping the box of books onto the floor. Together, we slipped into the back of the store, and he leaned in for a kiss, his arms wrapping around my body as he pulled me closer to him and pressed his lips to mine. We pulled apart when the little bell above the door jingled.

"Hey, Cass!" I heard from the front of the shop. I stepped through the curtain and saw May walking toward the counter.

"Hey May! Perfect timing. I was going to call you tomorrow, but since you're here now, I have a little surprise for you. I just received a box of books for the book drive, and the series you've been looking for was inside."

"Oh Cass, that's great!!" she sang as she grabbed two other books from the romance shelf and returned to the counter. "How much do I owe you for the series?"

"Those were in a box for the book drive, so whatever you would like to donate. That's where the money is going. I think I'm going to dedicate a shelf or two in here for the fundraiser. That way if the weather gets bad, the donations will still come in. Plus, the back storage area is almost full," I giggled.

"That's great! I, of course, will drop in a couple donations for you as well. My ladies are knitting up a storm." May was such a sweet lady, we had become good friends over the last couple of years. She owned the knitting shop down the road. I had wandered into her shop when I first moved here and was desperately looking for a hobby. I took a couple beginners how-to-knit classes with her until I concluded I was better at knotting the yarn as opposed to making those nice knitted designs. She pulled a fifty from her purse and handed it to me. "For the charity love."

"Thanks, May, it means so much to me."

"I know it does, dear. I know you're going to do very well. Now, how much do I owe you for the other two?" I rang up her purchase and was just finishing bagging her books when Ray came out front.

"Did you want me to close up tonight, Cass?" he asked, leaning against the doorway, shoving the remainder of a muffin in his mouth. "Let you get out of here a little early tonight?"

"Thanks, but I'm good, Ray. You may as well head home." Ray had worked all day at his garage, and he looked tired.

"Alright, I won't argue. Are you coming by tonight then?"

"Somewhere between seven and seven thirty?"

Ray nodded at May. "See you then, Cass." He leaned

in to give me a warm kiss goodbye and headed out the front door, leaving May and me alone.

May gave me a knowing smile as I passed her the debit machine. "What's that look for?" I asked.

"He really likes you."

I could feel the heat rise to my cheeks. Ray and I had been dating for a little over a year. We started out as friends—he had helped me out greatly since I had moved here and started the store. He was my neighbor and had started coming around the first summer I moved into the little cottage Jackson and I had owned together. He spent a lot of time helping me clean up the property, and I had been grateful for the help. We started to spend time together, and finally, he had asked me out. I wasn't sure how far things would go between us, but I was choosing to take things as they came. He was quite a bit older than me which normally wouldn't have bothered me, but twenty years apart got you some strange looks.

"Really, May? You think so?"

She nodded and passed me back the debit machine. "Yes."

"He's a great guy. He's been super helpful around here, and well, whatever happens between us happens. We'll see."

"I've known Ray a long time, and I've never seen him so happy. I would even say, judging from the look on his face before he left, he may want to get a little more serious with you," May winked.

I didn't know what to say, I wasn't sure I would be capable of dealing with anything more than what we already had.

"Alright, lovely, I'll let you get closed up. It's going to be a busy few weeks with all the tourists arriving next week for the Christmas season, then the book drive. Get yourself home and get some rest."

May grabbed her bag and headed out the front door. I waited the last five minutes, right until the clock read five before I locked up. I shut off the sign in the front window and started my nightly closing routine. It took me another half hour to count the till, quickly mop the floors, put the money in the safe, and make a shopping list for the store before I could leave.

The clock on the dashboard read seven as I pulled into the supermarket parking lot. I had already sent Ray a quick text as I was leaving the store to let him know I was running late. I grabbed my purse and headed across the parking lot to the front of the store.

I was wandering up and down every aisle, occasionally

stopping to check out items, my buggy getting fuller every aisle I walked down. I rounded the corner to the next aisle and ran into Maggie.

"Hey, Cass! You're in town late tonight. Everything okay?" she asked smiling.

"Yes, I just had to pick up a few things," I said, looking into my buggy. "Well, more than a few I guess. You were pretty busy today."

"Yes, I was planning to run over a coffee and fresh donut to you today, but I couldn't seem to get away. Maddy called in sick."

"Ah, that's okay. Thank you though. I hope it wasn't anything too serious."

"No, I don't think so."

"Well, I really should get going, I'm supposed to be having dinner with Ray tonight."

"Yes, me too, the kids are probably starving to death," Maggie laughed.

"I'm sure. Rebecca came into the store this morning and spent her allowance on books. Thought I would let you know."

"Well, at least it's on something other than video games. Oh, speaking of which, I had someone stop in the shop the other night and sign up to volunteer for the book drive."

"Oh, that's great, do you remember their name?"

"Well, off the top of my head I can't remember his name, he is actually one of Coldhaven Fire's new hires."

"Oh, I didn't know they were taking on anyone else."

"He told me he was a transfer, a young guy, really handsome. About five-ten, dark brown hair, crystal blue eyes, five o'clock shadow, and a body, girl, you should have seen. I'd give anything to be able to spend the night with that. I think his name was Brady or Bobby, something close to that, anyway."

A funny feeling came over me—she had described Brody, but it couldn't have been him. There was no way he was here, he wouldn't dare, would he?

"Cass? Are you alright?"

I said nothing, I barely heard her speak to me. I just stood staring ahead, tears coming to my eyes.

"Cass?"

After she said my name three more times and my phone vibrated in my pocket, I finally came back to where I was.

"Are you alright?"

"Hmmm, yes. Sorry. I'm fine. I have to go." I didn't give her another chance to ask me if I was alright. I walked away in a rush, taking my cart straight to the cashier. I had to get home.

Once I got everything loaded into the car, I climbed into the driver's seat and just sat there, my heart pounding. I was still slowly healing from everything that had happened, and even though it had been almost three years, I still wasn't completely healed. To be honest, I probably never would be. I closed my eyes, praying Maggie had been mistaken, and she had described someone else. After everything, things were finally starting to go as well as I imagined they were going to go from here on out. If Brody was truly back, I had a feeling this Christmas was going to be pure hell, just like the last few years.

Chapter Three

BRODY

I drove through the streets of Greyfield. Not much had changed since I left, it seriously looked as if time had stood still. I turned onto Oak Street and drove slowly down the road. The last time I had driven down this street was the night I left, running like the coward I was, in the early morning hours, away from the best thing that had ever happened to me. I wished I had been able to see it then. Instead, I had let so much time pass, I really felt it may be too late. A girl like Cass was probably remarried by now, and the bastard who got her would be the luckiest guy in the world. But I still felt the need to try.

I pulled up outside the old two-story red brick house

and just sat there. At first, I wasn't even sure I should turn the engine off, but I did. I couldn't help remembering the last time I had been in that house. It had been the day of that big fire down at the old factory. Cass had panicked when she couldn't get hold of me, and I rushed to get to the house. I had left my cell phone at the station, and when I got out of the shower and checked my messages, I knew she was worried. I drove as fast as I could, and as I approached her front door, she came flying out of the house right into my arms, almost knocking me over. I could almost see her running out that front door right now.

That was the night that virtually ended us if there ever was an *us*. As much as I wanted to forget, my heart wouldn't let me. Instead, I remembered everything about it, the wound still so fresh like it happened yesterday.

Brody - Three years earlier

"Whoa, Cass, what is it?"

"You can't leave me," she sobbed into my chest as tears

fell down her cheeks.

"Cass, baby, calm down." I wrapped my arms around her, taking her back into the house and shutting the door. "What has you so worked up?" I asked, brushing the loose strands of hair from her tear-covered face and looked into her watery eyes.

"Josie, she told me there were two firefighters missing at the fire. I tried to text you, but you didn't respond. I was afraid it was you." She sniffled, wiping her eyes with the palms of her hands.

"Babe, you know I don't take my phone on calls, I left it in my locker." I pulled her back against my chest, holding her tight, rubbing her arms to warm them. She let a tiny moan escape her lips. I placed two fingers under her chin and gently lifted her head. I slowly leaned down, hesitating at first until my lips gently brushed hers, sending a wave of pleasure through my body. She backed away, but then leaned back into me, placing her hand on my cheek, inviting me in for another kiss. This time her lips met mine with force, and I gently pried her lips open, gently sweeping my tongue through her mouth.

I shrugged out of my coat, letting it fall to the floor as I grabbed hold of her, lifting her so she could wrap her legs around my waist, my hands locking under her ass. I carried her over to the couch and sat down while she straddled my lap. As I kissed her deeply, I reached for the blanket at the end of the couch wrapping her in it—she was so cold.

We continued to kiss, and as I ran my hands over her body, I could feel my arousal growing. It was when I felt her grind against me that almost did me in. I tilted her head to the side to expose her neck and started kissing her, while my other hand ran down the outside of her shirt, cupping her breast. I rubbed my thumbs over her hardened nipples, another moan escaping her lips.

I quickly shifted out from under her, lifting her up and laying her down on the couch. I lay on her, grinding into her as I kissed her harder. I was crazy with want and desire.

She put her hands on my chest, pushing me back. I didn't listen to her plea, instead I kissed down her neck, and ran my hands down to the button on her jeans. I fumbled with it for a minute, then flicked it open, my fingers dancing along her waist.

"Brody," she whispered.

"I want you, Cass, I've wanted you for so fucking long, and now that I've had you, you're like a damn drug, I can't get enough of you."

"Brody, please." She gripped my hand, stopping me from exploring her body any further.

I stopped, a little worried, and studied the look in her eyes. I wanted her, fuck I wanted her, and I could see the want in her eyes too, but something was stopping her.

"Baby, just relax." I slowed my pace. Kissing her slower, my hands caressing her body. I unzipped her pants and slid my hand inside her panties. Running my fingers through her wet center, I started running circles over her clit. She moaned into my mouth, arching her back as I kissed her deeply. When she was just about to cum, I stopped kissing her and watched her face. I wanted to watch her come undone, but again, she reached down and grabbed my hand stopping me.

"Brody, please stop."

I instantly stopped, taking my hand away. I wasn't sure why she had stopped me this time, but when she opened her eyes, the look she gave me was not the one she had given me before—this one showed nothing but fear and uncertainty. I pushed myself up off her, turning away and headed over to the door.

"Brody, wait," she called from behind me.

"I'm sorry Cass. I don't know what came over me." I stood still for a moment, adjusting myself, then I turned to look at her, but she instantly averted her eyes.

I placed my hand on the doorknob and was just about to leave when her hand gripped my arm.

"Brody, wait, it's not that I don't want..."

"I've got to go." I felt like I was drowning. I had made a stupid mistake by ever getting into bed with her.

I heard her calling me as I crossed the street toward my house, but I didn't turn around, I couldn't. I had to get away. I couldn't believe what had happened between us over the past few weeks, I didn't know what had come over me. I had promised myself I would never act on my feelings for her. As soon as I was safely inside my house and the door was shut, I leaned against it and looked around the main floor of my house. I had run before after Jackson and Cass had gotten married.

We had been friends through college. I had crushed on her all through school, and at times, I thought Jackson had known it, but I could never be too sure. He finally asked her out, the same day I was planning to. Of course, I never said anything, and I don't think he ever knew how I truly felt about them. I tried to deal with it, but after they got married, I couldn't stay. I ran and got a job up in Canada. Lately, running was looking like a great option again.

Sure, I had promised him I would be here for her, but I was letting those feelings I had worked so hard to leave behind get in the way again, for real this time. We had been sleeping together for a little over a month, and things had changed between us. I couldn't do this to her, my feelings for her ran so deep, and I was afraid. She had just lost Jackson a year ago—what had I been thinking, making a move? I was foolish to think she would be ready to get involved with anyone, let alone me.

My phone pinged. Grabbing it from my pocket, I saw a message from Cass waiting on my phone.

Cass: Brody, please come back

I closed my eyes, gripping my phone in my hand. It

would be easier to walk away than to deal with having to see her. The hardest part of leaving would be knowing she truly needed me. I read the next message she sent—she was practically begging me to come back so we could talk.

I walked over and threw myself down on the couch and ran my hands through my hair. I typed out a response to her and sat with my thumb over the send button, debating telling her exactly how I felt, but I couldn't do it. I deleted everything I had just typed and sat there staring at her message, another one coming through, followed by another one.

I quickly sent a text to my landlord, got up and climbed the stairs to my bedroom. I grabbed a couple duffel bags from the closet, packed up the few clothes and small items I had, and went back downstairs. Then I sat down at the table with a piece of paper and a pen. Before I started writing, I sent off a short message to my boss in Canada to see if there was any work available. They were always looking for volunteer firefighters. Within minutes, I received my answer, and that was when I picked up the pen and started thinking about what to tell Cass.

As I wrote, my phone kept pinging, receiving messages from her, reading every one—I felt like a total ass not answering her. The last message she sent let me know she was going to bed and would see me in the morning. It ended with a crying face emoji which made me feel like the son-of-a-bitch I was by doing this to her, but I was at a loss, I didn't know what else to do. I folded the letter and set it on the table. I cleaned the mountain of dishes that sat in the sink, washing and drying them all and putting them away in the cupboard, something I never did. Once the place was cleaned, I glanced at my watch and saw it was almost two in the morning. I looked around grabbing the last few things that belonged to me out of the fully furnished house I had rented and headed out to my truck. I threw everything into the back and went back into the house, shutting off all the lights. Walking to the door, I looked around.

"Please forgive me, Jackson, I know I promised you, but everything considered, I just can't," I whispered. I opened the front door and locked it behind me. As I went to walk down the stairs, I looked across the street at the dark house, hoping Cass was asleep.

"I'm sorry, Cass, but I can't do this anymore. I love you," I whispered to the house, tears clouding my vision. I walked down the front steps and climbed into my truck. The engine roared to life, and I hoped she didn't hear it and wake up. I drove slowly down the driveway, keeping my eyes glued to her bedroom window, but tonight, the light didn't come on like it had so many others. I drove slowly down the street and came to the stop sign. I looked in my rear-view mirror, fighting between knowing this was the right thing for me to do and knowing it was the wrong thing for her, and in the end, I was going to break her heart, let alone my own. She had come to depend on me so much. I sat at that stop sign for five minutes, maybe ten before I finally made the decision to turn that corner, and as I drove away from the street that had been my home for the last year, I prayed, in time, she would forgive me, and she would be okay.

Brody - Present Day

The sound of a car door shutting finally jarred me from my memory. I blinked and looked toward the house I sat in front of. Everything was different. I frowned, it looked like new windows had just been put in, and two brand new cars sat in the driveway. The front porch had been painted. I climbed out of my truck and walked around to the driveway entrance, finally seeing the mailbox at the end of the driveway. In big white letters, the name Smith was painted on the front.

"Can I help you?" I heard a man's voice call. I looked up and saw an older man coming toward me from the detached garage in the back.

"I'm looking for an old friend who used to live here, Cass Reilly."

"Nope, sorry, don't know anyone by that name," he smiled.

"She used to own this place."

"Well, we just moved here a couple months ago, bought it off a guy by the last name of Davis."

"Do you know how long the previous owner may have lived here?"

"No, I'm sorry. I sure hope you haven't traveled a long way."

"Long enough. Do you happen to know where the previous family may have moved to?"

"I'm sorry, I don't."

"Okay, well, thanks." I frowned, looking up at the house. I could almost see her in the upstairs window, looking down on me like I had caught her doing so many times.

"Well, I hope you find your friend."

"Thanks. Sorry to bother you."

"It's no bother."

I took another long look at the house, nodded at the man who stood in front of me, and walked back to my truck. Maybe this was fate's way of telling me I needed to move on. I climbed back into my truck, started the engine, and pulled away from the curb, heading to my next stop.

Chapter Four

Cass

I fought tears all the way home. As soon as I pulled into my driveway, I called Ray to cancel tonight. I felt awful to start, but when I heard the disappointment in his voice, it magnified that feeling. After hearing what Maggie had told me, I was in no mood to spend time with anyone. I don't really know why I was so worked up, I couldn't even be sure it was him. If it was indeed Brody who had wandered into the coffee shop, I wondered if he had been looking for me. He would think I was still down in Grey-field, but if he wandered into the bookstore anytime soon, he would find me, and honestly, I wasn't sure I wanted to see him.

With the weight of having to see Ray off my shoulders, I grabbed all the bags from the back seat and went into the house, dropping them on the kitchen counter. I stopped and looked around. I felt completely depleted and just wanted my wine and my pajamas, but I still had to get wood in for the fire. I knew I should have done it this morning as snow was already starting to fall, and the cottage didn't hold the heat very well anymore. With the steady fall in the temperature outside, I knew I would need the extra warmth tonight. Once I had started the fire and put away the groceries, I took the now cold container of Chinese I had picked up for dinner and threw it in the microwave.

With food in hand, I turned on the TV to keep me company while I ate. I ran through the channels and finally found a movie to watch which started at nine. After I was done eating and had put my plate in the dishwasher, I made my way down to my bedroom to get changed. I found Missy, my cat, curled up on the end of the bed. She followed me out of the bedroom to the kitchen while I poured myself a glass of wine, dancing around my slippered feet until I got her some food which she attacked viciously.

I took my glass and the remainder of the bottle of wine with me into the living room where I curled up on the couch with a blanket and a couple of pillows while waiting for the movie to start. I glanced at the picture that sat on the end table. It was a picture of Jackson and me the last summer he had been alive. We were sitting together on a rockface, taking a rest after we had hiked through the mountains. His arms were wrapped around me, his face nuzzled into my neck. I remembered that day like it had been yesterday, yet so much had happened in the interim.

I stared at the photo, tears coming to my eyes. I knew he would be disappointed in me. Everything had changed with me, including the fact I still wasn't celebrating Christmas—it used to be my favorite time of year. The only Christmas I celebrated was at the store, the house remained bleak and undecorated. Since he had left me, I had managed to celebrate one Christmas, and that was the same Christmas Brody had left me. I picked up the frame and studied the picture.

"Man, I miss you so! Merry Christmas, Baby. I promise you this year I'll try to get a tree and perhaps begin to enjoy the season. I've been so lost without you, especially after Brody left me too. With him around, I always felt like I still had some part of you. I wish you would give me a sign to let me know I'll be okay." The tears were rolling down my cheeks now. "Did I tell you I've organized a book drive at the store to help the families of the fallen firefighters in this town? I'm worried Jackson, worried things won't go well. I know what you would tell me—just put my best foot forward, and it will work out. You always said that. You always believed in me even when

I didn't believe in myself. I know I've let you down, you never wanted me to give up writing, but I didn't have a choice." I felt ridiculous sitting here talking to a photograph. I put the picture back down, wiped the tears running down my cheeks, and drank down the remainder of the wine in my glass. I grabbed the bottle from the table and poured another glass, finally turning to the sappy Hallmark Christmas movie which would certainly end with me in tears on the couch.

I was just about to head to the washroom before the movie started when I saw I had an email from my friend Rebecca, a fellow author.

Dearest Cass,

I hope this email finds you well. I know you haven't really been writing, but I wanted to reach out to you with an opportunity, anyway. A few of us have come up with an idea for an anthology, and we would love it if you would consider joining us. I will forward the details once I know you are interested. Please respond ASAP, we would love to have your name included in this project.

Rebecca

I bit my bottom lip and reread her email. Perhaps this was the boost I needed to get back out there in a world I had loved. I smiled as I typed out a quick yes and laid my phone down on the table.

I got up and ran to the washroom and grabbed a snack from the kitchen before sitting back down with my wine. I was about twenty minutes into the movie when my phone pinged with a message. I picked it up, hoping it was Rebecca with the information about this anthology but was pleasantly surprised to see Josie's name flash across my screen. I smiled to myself, I hadn't talked to Josie in a while, and I missed her.

Josie: You around?

Me: Hey! Miss you!

Josie: Me too. Don't have long to chat, I'm hiding in the bathroom but wanted to let you know Brody is here.

I almost choked on my mouthful of wine as I read her text. Brody. So, it very well could have been him at the coffee shop. My stomach did a sudden flip.

Me: What does he want?

Josie: He's looking for you. He wants to see you. Did you want me to tell him where you are?

I stared at my phone, my hand shaking. Until today, I had done my best to put him to the back of my mind because it was the only way I could move on from what had happened between us. But having heard his name twice today, after it had been so long since I had even thought about him, was making me crazy.

Josie: Are you there, Cass?

Me: Just tell him I moved. That's it. You haven't heard from me since I left.

That killed me to type, but I was still so angry and hurt after how he left. Plus, I was just starting to get on with my life here—with the store and with Ray. I guess you could say I was as happy as I could be with my new life. But if truth be told, I still had feelings for him. Feelings that would never go away. To be honest, I was afraid if I saw him, it would open everything back up, and once again, my heart would belong to him.

Josie: He really misses you.

Me: Please, Josie, just cover for me.

Josie: Okay, Cass. If you say so. I'll do my best.

Me: Thanks Josie.

I threw my phone down on the coffee table and placed my head in my hands. Missy jumped up and made herself comfortable in my lap. Petting her head, I tried to turn my attention back to the movie on the TV but found it increasingly difficult with thoughts of Brody running through my head. Sure, over the last couple of years I had gotten a few random texts from him, but I never had the heart to answer—some, I never even had the heart to read.

I got up from the couch, laying Missy off to the side and walked down to my bedroom, grabbing my memory box off the dresser, and went back to my spot on the couch. I very rarely went into the box, the memories in there too much for me to handle most days. Taking a deep breath, I opened the box. There it sat, staring up at me, my name in Brody's handwriting on the back of a wrinkled envelope. I picked up the envelope, running my thumb over it, instantly being transported back to that dreadful day.

Cass - Three years earlier

I sat down and cried my heart out. I wanted to be with him, I was in love with him, but I was so afraid to get involved again. I wished he would have let me explain myself. I spent the night worrying to the point I was sick. I had sent Brody a couple of texts and even tried to call him, but every attempt ended the same—unanswered. At four, I looked out my bedroom window over at his house. His truck was gone, and the house sat in darkness. I was afraid something had happened, and he got called out to an emergency, so I sent him another text and laid back down in bed.

By ten, I was tired of being ignored, so I threw my boots on and marched across the street. We were supposed to leave for the cottage today. There was no way he could ignore me if I was standing at his front door.

I marched up the front steps and pounded hard on the door. There was no answer. I grabbed my keys out of my pocket and inserted the spare key he had given me into the lock. The door squeaked open, the house quiet.

"Brody?" I called, stepping inside.

Everything was in place. I looked out the side window and saw his truck still wasn't in the driveway. I frowned to myself but made my way into the kitchen. The pile of clean dishes that always sat in the drain pan was gone, everything had been put away.

I grabbed a piece of paper off the notepad that hung on the fridge and was just about to scribble out a note for him when I saw an envelope with my name scribbled in his handwriting.

I frowned, picking up the envelope. I opened it and removed the piece of paper inside, a sinking feeling settling over me.

My Dearest Cass,
You're probably wondering by now where I am. I'm sorry to do this. I'm letting myself down, I'm letting Jackson down, but most importantly, I'm letting you down. It's not okay, I know. I hope you'll understand, Cass and find a way to forgive me because I will never be able to forgive myself. My feelings for you have grown, in case you hadn't noticed, and I don't know what to do about it. It's not supposed to be this way, Cass. I'm going to try to sort out these feelings and get

*over you so I can come back and do what Jackson's asked
of me.*
Love, Brody.

I could barely contain the shake running through my body, the shake and the cold of extreme stress. I needed him, more than he knew, and if he had of just talked to me or been a little more receptive last night, he might have found out I loved him too.

I pulled my cell phone from my pocket and dialed my mom. I needed someone. As soon as I knew she was on her way, I folded the letter and held it tightly in my hand. The shaking was getting so bad, I barely trusted my legs to carry me back home, but they did, all the way back home and upstairs to bed where I spent the next few months.

To be honest, I really couldn't remember how long I had been there because I lost count. That letter had almost ended me.

With tears pouring down my cheeks, I read and reread that old crinkled letter. Crinkled because I had read it every day and night for almost a year after he had gone. But tonight, I let all of those feeling from that day come back to me. It didn't matter how long he had been gone, the feelings were still there, and they were still very raw. I picked up my phone and opened a text window to Josie. The blinking cursor flashing, I started to type and erased, again staring at that blinking cursor.

Every fiber of my being wanted to tell her to tell him where I was, to tell him to come see me, to come home and repair my heart, but I was afraid to type those words. They just wouldn't come despite how my heart felt. I wiped the tears from my eyes, put the phone back down, gently fold the crinkled old letter, placed it back in its envelope, put the envelope back into my memory box, closed the lid, and placed the little lock back on the front. Locking back up what was left of that part of my heart, or so I hoped. I poured myself another glass of wine, took a deep cleansing breath, and curled up under the warm blankets, pulling Missy close and turned what little attention I had left back to the movie.

Chapter Five

BRODY

I spent the night at Bryan and Josie's. They invited the old crew over, and we spent the night drinking and laughing. I had just gotten back into Coldhaven after the long two-hour drive from Greyfield. I pulled off the highway and drove past the only local mechanic shop Coldhaven had to offer, Ray's Garage. If Cass did live around here, this would be the only place she would go for her car to be repaired. Most mechanics knew everyone in small towns. So, I pulled into the closest driveway and turned my truck around. It wouldn't be a loss because I needed to book in for an oil change and have my winter tires put on, anyway.

I pulled my truck into an empty spot and shut the engine off.

Walking into the only open dock bay door, I looked around the garage. A car was up on the lift, but the shop was empty, a mess of tools laying on the nearby workbench. I wandered into the small office just off to the left. It was empty as well; a mess of papers covered the small desk. "Hello," I called into the shop. All was quiet, but then I heard the toilet flush.

"What can I help you with?" A man stepped out from a door off to the back left of the building, wiping his hands on a dirty towel.

"I need to book an appointment to have my oil changed and my winter tires put on."

"Sure thing." I watched as he pulled his phone out of his pocket and started checking dates. "I can book you in a couple weeks from now, say the thirtieth."

I nodded and put the appointment in my calendar.

"Hey, I was wondering if you could help me with something else. I'm looking for an old friend, Cass Reilly. She used to have a cottage up in this area, and I was wondering if you could tell me if she's living in Coldhaven now?"

He took a couple steps forward, inching closer to me, his steely eyes running over me like he was sizing me up.

"Who wants to know?"

"Brody Thompson," I said, holding my hand out for him to shake, only he didn't shake it. He just stood there studying me, not saying anything.

"Well, Brody Thompson, there is something you should know. People around these parts just don't go sharing with strangers if they know where someone is."

"Look, she's a close friend of mine, I'd like to see her."

"I'm sure you would, but if she were as close of a friend as you say, you would know where she was, wouldn't you? Truthfully, I'd love to help you, and if I knew anyone by that name, I might be able to, but I don't." He looked at the crest on the breast of my jacket. "So, you work for our fire department, do you?"

"I do."

"I know lots of guys in the department, why don't I know you?"

"I was just transferred here."

"I see. Well, Brody, I'm sorry I couldn't help you more, but I don't know your friend, and I know everyone in this town."

I watched him for a bit as he went back to work on the car on the lift. I had a sinking feeling he was lying to me.

"Is there anything else I can help you out with?" he grunted.

I didn't answer his question, I didn't like liars. Crossing my arms, I stood watching him for a few seconds. "I'll drop my truck off on the thirtieth." I turned around and headed back to my truck.

I had an inkling she was living at the cottage she and Jackson had bought. I didn't want to just show up on her doorstep, but if it came down to it, I would have no choice. Regardless, I couldn't do anything about it now, I had a few days left of work and had to continue my search for an apartment. Until I found one, I would be living at the station.

Cass

I was so glad to see Ray when he walked through the back door of the store after he had closed his shop for the day. I'd been so busy, I'd barely had enough time for a quick coffee, let alone lunch. I was busy putting away my shipment of new stock when he came up behind me, wrapping his arms around my waist.

"Hey, you have anything to eat today?" he asked, kissing me on the cheek, his strong hands gripping my waist, "You're getting a little thin."

"Yes, of course, there are still some cookies in the back, along with coffee if you want anything."

"Cass, I swear your diet consists of nothing but cookies and coffee," he laughed, taking the handful of books I was holding and putting them on the cart. He turned me around and pulled me into him.

"Pretty much, but if it weren't for cookies, I wouldn't have eaten today, so there is that. And I feel I should pay you somehow, lord knows you won't take money for all the time you've put in here."

"Really, Cass, you're my girlfriend, it's not a big deal, I'd just go home to an empty house until you get home. Besides, I don't mind helping you out. Now, I'm going to go and grab a cookie and coffee before I start helping you with the next box." He leaned down and kissed me before he headed to the kitchen.

As soon as Ray disappeared into the back, a few customers trickled in and started to browse. I busied myself helping them find what they were looking for and as soon as the last customer left the store, I immediately went back to stocking the shelves, cracking open the last box of books I had ordered.

"Oh, Cass, I meant to tell you," Ray said, coming around the corner, carrying a mug of hot coffee. "Some guy stopped by the shop today, wondering if you lived around here."

I frowned, swallowing hard, thinking back to last night's message from Josie and of course, talking to Maggie.

"Really?" I hadn't told Ray about them—come to think about it, I had never mentioned Brody to Ray, at all. All he knew was I was widowed.

"Yeah, no worries though, I acted as if I didn't know you," he winked, stuffing the last of the chocolate chip cookie in his mouth. "Now, why don't you go and have a sit-down and something other than refined sugar to eat, I can handle things out here." He grabbed the handful of books I was holding in my hand.

"You sure?"

"Positive. Go, I'll call you if I need you."

Grabbing my lunch from the little fridge, I sat down at the small table in the lunchroom and unwrapped the sandwich I had brought. It wasn't much, but it was something. I took a bite and grabbed my phone from my purse. I reread the texts from Josie and typed out a message to her.

Me: How did it go last night? Did he believe you?

Josie: I tried, Cass, I told him I hadn't heard from you. I'm not sure he believed me

Me: What makes you think that?

Josie: Because he said he didn't believe me.

I chuckled—such a typical Josie response.

Me: Thanks, Josie, I'll call you later.

I sighed but continued to laugh at her response. I missed her so, she was always so much fun to be around. I made a mental note to give her a call later in the week and maybe arrange a visit with her and the family.

The rest of the afternoon was quiet and went by smoothly. Thanks to Ray, I ended up getting the whole new shipment put away while he started clearing the shelves for the book drive. I wanted to start collecting whatever I could, and I was happy to be able to concentrate on nothing but sales for the rest of the week. I had shut the open sign off in the front window and was going to help the last couple of customers in the shop. Ray came out from the back carrying a couple of boxes of the books that were donated and started placing them on the shelf.

"You want these in any particular order?" he asked as he walked over to the empty shelves.

"Whatever you do is fine." I would have plenty of time tomorrow to arrange things how I wanted. What mattered to me right now was they at least got filled. "Just make sure any doubles are put together."

"I can do that. Did you want to come to my place tonight for dinner? I was going to pick up a pizza on the way home," Ray asked as he collapsed the last box he had emptied.

"Sure, that sounds great," I answered as I locked up the door behind the last customer.

"Alright, I'm going to head out and let you finish. I'll pop over and feed Missy for you as well."

"Sounds good. Thank you."

By the time I pulled into Ray's driveway, it was close to six-thirty. Ray greeted me at the door, pulling me in for a kiss, then stepped aside to let me in.

"Smells great, I'm starved," I said as my stomach let out a large growl. I threw my coat on the back of the chair by the door and followed Ray into the kitchen.

"So, I went over to feed Missy."

"Great thank you."

"Who's the handsome guy in the picture with you on the end table?" he asked grabbing two plates from the cupboard.

I took in a deep breath. I normally kept that picture of Jackson and me in my bedroom, but I must have forgotten to put it away.

"That was my husband."

Ray stopped what he was doing and turned to face me. "He was a good-looking guy."

"I know I haven't told you much about him other than he passed away."

"No, you haven't."

"He was a firefighter. They were fighting a fire in an apartment building just outside of Greyfield. He was doing search and rescue on the fifth floor. They had reports two people were still inside, so he went in. It was just a routine part of his job he had done thousands of times. He was on the last floor, at the last two apartments. He took a step, and the floor collapsed under him, and he fell two floors. When he fell, he hit his head and cracked his helmet. He suffered smoke inhalation, and when they found him, he was unconscious. He was rushed to the hospital where they decided to keep him overnight for observation. I stayed with him for most of the evening, but he was adamant I go home. He went into cardiac arrest later that night and passed away. He's my inspiration why I wanted to do this book drive. When those families lost their loved ones in that fire last summer, I felt a strong need to give back. I know what that kind of loss is like first-hand, and it breaks my heart to know every one of those men had young kids who will grow up without their dads."

"Oh, Cass, I had no idea."

"Don't be silly, of course, you didn't know," I smiled, trying to make him feel comfortable again.

"So, is that when you gave up your writing career?"

"It was around that time, yes. I was just drowning. But I got an email the other night. I was approached by an author friend of mine, and they are working on an anthology. They want me to join them and write something for it. I told them I would do it."

"Do you think that's a good idea?"

"Honestly, yes, it would be a good comeback for me. I could re-cover and publish all my other books again, rebrand myself, and get back out there."

"What about the store?"

"Well, I'd still do that, of course, until, you know, things pick up for me. I used to be pretty popular."

"I see. I just don't see how you can do both, Cass. I think you're taking on too much."

I had been so excited about this, but I instantly quieted down. How one person could deflate you in an instant was beyond me. But at the sign of his displeasure, that was exactly how I felt, completely deflated, instead of supported.

"I don't know what I was thinking. I guess I'll see how it goes, but you're probably right."

"I know I am, you'll see. You barely have time now for anything. And you can't afford to hire anyone at the shop. I saw your books, I know."

I hung my head as he passed me my plate and a can of pop and opened the pizza box, displaying a large pepperoni pizza with mushrooms. I grabbed two slices from the box and followed Ray into the living room. I honestly felt like I could cry. I had worked so hard, but the truth was, my passion just didn't lie with running the bookstore, and that was part of the problem. My passion was writing, and maybe if it took off for me again, I could get rid of the store or possibly keep both. Or maybe he was right, and I was being silly even thinking that.

We ate in silence, watching the news. Afterward, we sat on the couch in the quiet, talking about our day. When Ray finally became quiet, I checked the time on my watch.

"Ray, I should go, it's getting late." Truth was, I had wanted to leave as soon as he started putting me down, but I had sucked it up. I grabbed our plates and headed into the kitchen.

"You can just leave those on the counter. I'll take care of them."

"You sure? I don't mind washing them up."

"I'm positive."

I placed the dishes on the counter and headed to the front door, Ray following behind. He grabbed my coat from the hook, helping me put it on. I spun around and met Ray's chest. He reached out and grabbed my hair to pull it out of my jacket, grazing my neck with his fingers as he did so.

We stood for a moment, looking into one another's eyes, saying nothing. Ray slowly leaned in, getting closer and placed a soft kiss on my mouth. He pulled back a little, looking deeper into my eyes, placing his hands on my waist.

I bit my bottom lip. His eyes never leaving mine, he

leaned in again and kissed me again, deeper this time, pulling me against him. I wrapped my arms around his neck, his rough hands grazing my bare skin as my shirt rose.

"I'm sorry it was a bad day. Stay the night with me," he whispered as he pulled me against him tighter, deepening the kiss more, his hand running up my shirt, cupping my breast, brushing his thumb over my hardened nipple. I could feel his hardness pressing into my thigh. He continued his assault down my neck, slowly removing my jacket from my shoulders.

"I guess I could stay for a bit." I moaned as he met my mouth again. I let my jacket fall to the floor as he picked me up and carried me up the stairs toward the bedroom.

I stood outside Ray's front door. He kissed the top of my shoulder.

"Ray I have to get going, it's late. I still have a little work to get done tonight. I didn't have a lot of time at work today to get the outline for this book done, and I have a deadline to hit."

He kissed me again. "It's okay, I understand. Just would have been nice to fall asleep with you in my arms."

Even though he said it was okay, I could see the disappointment in his eyes as I looked at him. I leaned in and gave him a kiss and hug. He had just let me go, and I was about to start walking to my car when he spoke up.

"Cass, I really don't understand this need you have to write. Honestly, as I said, the bookstore should be enough."

"Ray, this was always my dream, I have to do this. I had it taken away from me, and it's rare you get second chances in this life. I can't let it pass me by." I wasn't going to stand here and argue with him or let him put me down anymore.

"Fine, whatever, go home get some rest," he said, clearing his throat.

I pressed the remote start Ray had installed for me. "Oh, before I forget, I need you to order me some new tires for winter."

"You'll be fine."

"My winters are five years old, Ray, they were getting really slippery last year."

"You barely go anywhere, they'll be fine."

With my head down, I walked toward my car, climbed into the front seat, and put my seatbelt on. I jumped when I felt my phone vibrate with a notification. I frowned, pulling it from my pocket. It was after midnight, and I was with the only person who would have messaged me unless there was an emergency. I glanced up and saw Ray had already shut the front door and shut the outside light off. Opening the messenger app, my breath hitched, a funny feeling coming over me as my heart started pumping hard. Tears filled my eyes as I read the message.

Brody: I need to see you. When is a good time?

Chapter Six

BRODY

When I returned from Greyfield the other night, the disappointment that hit me had been debilitating. I wanted so bad to find her—if she wasn't here, I had no clue where she could be. I had begged Josie to give me her number or at least confirm if I had the correct one, but she out and out refused. As the night progressed and Josie had turned in, I begged Bryan for her number. After promising him I would never speak a word of this to Josie, he confirmed I had the correct number.

Now that I knew I had the right number, I wished she would just respond and tell me to go away if she didn't want anything to do with me. I didn't know what to do.

Showing up on her doorstep may not be the wisest thing, but I needed to know the truth—it was going to be the only way I would be able to move on with my life.

The sun shone as I drove slowly down Main Street until I found a parking spot. Last night, my suspicions had been confirmed on my way back to the fire station. I happened to see her walking to her car, parked out behind Coldhaven Books. She had dropped a box into the back seat, then headed back inside.

I'd parked my truck across the street last night and watched her for a bit through the window. She was just as attractive as I remembered—her mid-length brown hair perfectly cut to frame her face, her dress snug against all her curves. She looked happy, but when the last customer left, once she had closed the store, a look of sadness came over her face. I had no idea why the hell she was working in a bookstore, she was a popular author, it should have been enough to support her. I watched as she worked on the window display, but the sadness in her eyes was almost unbearable for me to see. I decided to Google her name to see when her last release came out and was shocked to find the last release was before Jackson died. Which meant what she had been working on when I had left had never been released, possibly never even finished. There was barely any other information on her, her website was gone. It was like everything I remembered about her had vanished like it had been a dream. It was like she had just disappeared.

I figured maybe time away would help how I felt about her, but it did the exact opposite. Seeing her now had confirmed how awful I felt for leaving and just how deep my feelings for her ran. I still felt the same way for her as I had so long ago. I had tried burying myself in work and dating, I had even been in a relationship for two years, but all we did was argue. All I did was find faults with her and wonder what could have been if things had gone differently with Cass. There were so many times I wanted to kick myself in the ass for walking away from her. I should have come back to her, but I didn't—until now. It didn't help that I felt like I had betrayed my best friend. Even though he was gone, I still couldn't forgive myself for abandoning her when she needed me the most, and I hated the fact I wanted so much more with her than just to be her shoulder to lean on.

I was punishing myself in a sea of regret and had been since that night I drove away. It was enough, I had to do something about it. When I broke up with my last relationship, I started to crave Cass more, and now that she was within reach, it was like an itch I couldn't scratch. But I feared I would end up living with the repercussions of my choices, especially when she wouldn't respond to me.

I put my truck in park and shut the engine off. She had stepped away from the window, but the lights were still on in the store, the open sign still blinking so I figured she would still be there for a while. I wanted to go see her tonight but wasn't sure what I was going to say to her or if I even had the courage to go. I just knew I needed to. I needed to explain to her why I left. I needed her to find her forgiveness. Fuck, I needed her, and I was going to use whatever I had to get her back. If there was anything this time apart had taught me, it was that I was totally in love with her and nothing would ever lessen those feelings.

Instead of heading to the bookstore, I climbed out of the truck and walked across the street to the coffee shop. I needed to gather up some form of courage. As soon as I opened the door, the smell of coffee hit me. I walked up to the counter and waited to be served.

"Ah, Brody, right? How are you? Have you spoken to Cass yet?" the girl behind the counter asked.

I looked at her a little confused.

"About the book drive? She's still there. If you wanted to speak with her, you should do it now, she'll be closing soon. I mentioned to her you were going to volunteer," she said, nodding her head in the direction of the little bookstore.

I glanced across the street. All the lights were still on, and she was back working in the front window display. It was hard for me to take my eyes off her, she looked so beautiful. She finally reached up, and the illuminated open sign went dark.

"Well looks like it won't be tonight, looks like she just closed up for the night." I smiled at her. I breathed a sigh of relief. I felt like a total coward, I had been waiting for my out.

"Well, there's always tomorrow," she smiled and handed me my coffee.

"Always tomorrow." I thanked her, took the cup, and went to sit in the front window, watching Cass from my seat. She was still working away on the window display when suddenly, an older man approached her from behind. I frowned as he said something to her, causing her to smile. I was irritated and got my back up a little as he wrapped his arms around her and pulled her into him, a smile lighting up her face as he kissed her on the side of the neck. I could feel every muscle in my body tensing— it should be me over there, not him, and it would have been if I hadn't been such a coward. She walked away, leaving him in the window and disappeared from my sight.

I grabbed my coffee and headed across the street. I pretended to be looking at her Christmas display in the window, but what I really wanted was to get a closer look at this guy. I wanted to know who and what my potential competition was. At first glance, I didn't recognize him, but when he turned and faced the window, he looked very familiar. I searched my mind and studied his face, then it came to me. It was that fucking mechanic—the asshole lied to me. He was easily twenty or so years older than her. I could feel rage build in me at the memory of his words.

Before I did something completely stupid, I turned and headed in the direction of my truck before Cass came out from the back. I had been known to act irrationally at times and didn't want to get myself into trouble. Plus, I didn't want to come back into Cass's life acting that way to start. Instead, I sucked in a deep breath to try to calm down, climbed into my truck, and headed back to the firehouse.

Chapter Seven

Cass

The week had gotten progressively busier with the influx of tourists coming in for the ski season. It was Saturday afternoon, Ray had been busier than normal at the garage as well and hadn't had time to come by and help me out as much.

I was feeling defeated. I still didn't have many volunteers for the book sale, and I was desperately behind on my book for the anthology. The last few days Ray and I had been arguing, and he basically told me he wasn't going to support my venture back into my writing. Instead, he would pull me away from writing every single chance he got. I was trying not to stress out too much and was looking forward to getting home tonight to have some alone time and get some writing done. The phone rang just as I was about to shut the open sign off and start my weekly cleaning. Tomorrow was my day off, and I preferred the store ready for Monday morning before I left on Saturday night.

"Merry Christmas, Coldhaven Books, Cass speaking," I sang into the phone.

"Merry Christmas? It's only November," Ray chuckled.

"I'm just trying to get into the spirit early, I guess." I had little to none of it, anyway and dealing with the public you had to have some.

"I see. Well, I was wondering if maybe you'd like to catch a movie tonight in town? I can come by and pick you up if you like." Ray's deep voice poured over the phone.

"I guess, what's playing?" I let out a deep breath. I didn't feel as if I could say no, we normally used Saturday night as our date night since we were both closed on Sunday.

He chuckled into the phone. "Well, I'm pretty sure I saw that new Christmas movie you've been talking about is playing. Thought you might like to see that, it starts at six-thirty. Do you think you could be ready by then?"

I glanced at the clock and mentally calculated the time in my head. "It will be close, but I think I can be."

"Alright, I'm just about to close up here. I'm going to shower, swing by the theater, grab the tickets, then come get you."

"Sounds good. I'll see you soon." I hung up the phone and finished putting away the two boxes of used books that had been dropped off for the book drive. I had pretty much cleared out the set of shelves I had set aside for the drive today, so I wanted to get more books loaded for Monday. I quickly mopped the old wooden floors, finished counting the till, and was about to head back to the safe when I heard a gentle tap on the front door.

Bugged at the fact Ray should know better and enter in through the back, I turned to answer the door but stopped dead in my tracks as soon as I saw the face peeking in the window.

I couldn't believe my eyes. He stood at the door, dressed in a Coldhaven Fire Department jacket. I couldn't move from my spot, it felt like I was seeing a ghost. The last time I had seen him, he had been walking away from me, down the front steps of my house back in Greyfield, in a rush to get away, to leave me. In those couple of seconds our eyes met, everything came rushing back. The way it felt to be comforted by him after Jackson had died, all the secrets we had shared, the fear I had felt when he couldn't be reached after that big fire, the complete joy I had felt when he had come striding up my front steps after I thought the worst, the greatest sex I think I'd ever had, and the worst mistake I had made that drove him from my life. I was ashamed to admit, I still dreamed about that night, and after I woke, the anger and resentment I had felt when he left without a word, never to be seen or heard from again would always come creeping back in.

He held his hand up in a wave, a small smile coming to his lips, then he pointed to the door handle mouthing the words can I come in. I swallowed and took a hesitant first step forward, unsure whether my legs would hold me, or if I would fall to the ground. I turned the deadbolt and pulled the door open, the frigid cold hitting me in the face. Brody stepped inside and shut the door behind him.

"Is it really you?" I asked, swallowing the lump in my throat.

"It's really me, in the flesh. How have you been, Cass?" he asked, not taking his eyes from mine. In that instant, I had a moment of weakness. I just wanted to have him hold me in his arms, against his chest, and I wanted to tell him everything that had happened in the time we had been apart and beg him to make it better, but I couldn't. He couldn't be my weakness, I had to keep my guard up.

"You doing okay?"

"It's been a while. I'm doing well, how are you?"

"I'm alright." The air in the room was thick, and I could feel the tension mounting. "I was hoping that you would reply to the messages I sent you."

I looked at the ground, I was having a hard time

keeping it together. The scent of his cologne combined with his large muscular frame was making me feel weak.

"I'm sorry, I couldn't, I didn't exactly know what to say."

"I'm sorry to just show up like this, but I needed to see you. I have to tell you how sorry I am for what I did. For leaving."

We stood there, eyes locked on one another, his gaze burning into me. What did he expect me to say, it was all okay? When the truth was it was far from being okay?

I stood there frozen. I was afraid, afraid if I took my eyes off him even for a second, he would disappear again. I wanted to be excited and happy to see him, but since everything that had happened to me over the last three years had been a direct result of him leaving, it was a little hard. Despite the silence that hung between us, I didn't hear the back door open or Ray calling my name. I didn't hear his footsteps as he walked through the back of the store and came up behind me. I even jumped when I felt his strong hand squeeze my shoulders.

"Everything okay here, Cass?"

I took my eyes off Brody for an instant and turned my head to see Ray standing right behind me, in a rather protective stance. When I looked back at Brody, his gaze was fixed on Ray. I saw a look in Brody's eyes I had never seen before—jealousy, rage—I wasn't sure what it was, but

I didn't like it. I didn't need a fight in the middle of my store.

"Ray, it's okay. This is a friend of my husband. He was just passing through town and stopped in for a quick hello." It was the only lie I had to offer. I glanced at Brody, waiting for him to calm down and take his eyes off Ray, but he continued to study him closely.

Ray relaxed a bit but still stood behind me as if I needed protecting, his hands rubbing my shoulders, letting me know he was there. Finally, he leaned into me and whispered, "I have the tickets, we should get going. Movie is going to start in ten minutes." I knew he had done that to get Brody to leave.

I nodded, but when I turned to Brody to say something to him, his eyes were set on Ray's hands, still sitting on my shoulders. I now knew the look plastered on Brody's face was jealousy. I was just about to say something, but Brody beat me to it.

"I thought you didn't know her, Ray?" he said through clenched teeth.

I glanced from Ray to Brody, both men now glaring at one another. I stepped out from under Ray's hands and walked over to Brody who stood there, tense, avoiding my eyes, taking in slow, steady, controlled breaths. I placed my hand on his bicep.

"Brody, how about I call you later? When we can talk," I said, giving him an unsure smile. I had to get him out of here. If I didn't, there was no doubt in my mind, there was going to be a fight. I knew Ray, he didn't back down from much of anything, and neither did Brody.

"No, Cass, I want to know why Ray here didn't tell me the truth. I asked him if he knew you," he said, taking a step closer to Ray, pushing himself against me. I felt a surge of excitement run through me as his hard chest pushed into my small frame.

"Buddy, look, the lady wants you to leave. I suggest you take a hike before I remove you," Ray bit out, squaring up to Brody.

I closed my eyes and took in a deep breath. Jackson had always told me Brody could have a temper when he wanted. I had never seen it before, but I knew he had been right. At this point, I knew he certainly didn't need to be provoked. Ray may have been bigger, but I knew Brody could take him. Jackson had told me too many stories, and Brody was almost twenty years younger after all.

"Ray, could you leave us for a moment," I asked harshly.

I didn't look at Ray, just kept my focus on Brody, listening for Ray to leave. I knew when we were alone—Brody had visibly started to calm down. I glanced over my shoulder to make sure Ray had indeed left the room.

"Cass, please, for the love of God, tell me you're not dating this guy? He's got to be twenty years older than you. I mean is he even able to get it up?"

"Brody, please, can I call you later? We can talk then, get reacquainted."

He studied my face. "Sure, answer my question first."

I didn't say anything, just stood and looked into his blue eyes. They were darker than I remembered, maybe it was because he was angry, but they were still the same blue eyes I had loved to get lost in. Brody came closer and brushed a loose strand of hair from my eyes, his warm, strong hand cupping my cheek as he looked down into my eyes. I could feel the heat from his breath on my cheek.

"Cass, just answer me, I need to know," he whispered.

Placing my hands on his chest, I could feel his strong tense muscles underneath his shirt. "We've been seeing one another for about a year," I whispered. "Now, please, I'll call you later."

Brody's looked back to the curtain that separated the front of the store from the back. "Am I too late, Cass?"

I frowned, I didn't know what he was talking about, and I wasn't sure if I should ask, but my curiosity got the best of me.

"Too late for what?" My voice was low, the last thing I wanted was for Ray to come out here.

"Fuck it." He leaned forward and gently pressed his lips to mine, pulling me into his embrace. I closed my eyes, kissing him back—I had been dreaming for the last three years about this kiss. He took hold of both my hands and wrapped my arms around his neck, running his hands down the side of my body, his thumbs grazing the sides of my breasts, finally resting his hands on my hips as he deepened the kiss, forcing my lips open, sweeping his tongue through my mouth. It was exactly how I'd remembered, maybe better, and as his teeth grazed my bottom lip and his tongue swept across mine again, I felt my knees go weak. My body was on fire—he had awakened parts of me with his kiss that had been dead since he left. When his lips had been on mine, I felt completely whole, but as he pulled away from me, I felt completely empty and lost. He looked over my shoulder, toward the back of the building, smirked, then looked down into my eyes.

"Call me tonight. I plan to fight for you Cass, but judging from your reaction to that kiss, I'm not going to have to fight too hard even if you've been with him for a while, and remember, I have a sexual appetite you can't quench, I can go for hours, in case you've forgotten," he whispered into my mouth, kissing me one more time.

I remembered all too well as I watched him walk across the street toward his truck, the little bell over the door bringing me back to reality.

"So, he's finally gone, are you ready to go?" I didn't answer him I just locked the door quickly. "Cass, is everything okay?" I felt his hands on my shoulders as I watched Brody pull away from the curb.

I nodded, I didn't trust my voice, so I swallowed hard before answering.

"Yep. Let me grab my purse and coat." I shrugged, pulling away from him. I reached up to wipe the tears away before turning around. I had no idea I was even crying. I grabbed my purse, and we left from the back door. The last thing I wanted to do was go and watch a movie, I really wanted to take my car and head home. But since Ray had already bought the tickets, how could I say no? The phone call I wanted to make tonight would have to wait.

Chapter Eight

Cass

I pulled into the driveway and sat in the car, waiting for the garage door to open. When I had been married, not a Christmas went by without the house being decorated in outdoor lights. There was a time, I would have already been driving Jackson crazy about getting a tree. I parked the car in the garage and walked into the house, throwing my purse on the counter and looked around. There was nothing that would say Christmas was just around the corner. I should have had this whole place decorated by now. Regardless, I was happy to finally be home. It had been a long and emotional day, and I was exhausted. Even though the movie was good, and it had been a nice break, it seemed to go on and on. I was ready to head home, but Ray wanted to take me out for a bite to eat. At first, I refused, but my stomach gave me away, letting out a large groan at the mention of pizza.

While we ate, he kept asking me questions about Brody. I really wasn't ready to talk about him, and I was pissed Ray would have lied to anyone who came around looking for me. I really wanted to ask him why he would do that, but I just didn't have the energy to get into any sort of argument or discussion about any of it tonight.

The conversation between us died after we left the restaurant. I sat quietly, looking out the window as Ray drove back to the store so I could get my car. Just as I was about to get out of the car, Ray cleared his throat.

"Why don't you come back to my place tonight, spend the night with me?" he asked, placing his hand on my knee before I got out of the car.

I kept my head turned away from him. I didn't know how to tell him I wanted to be alone.

"Cass?"

"I think I'm going to go home tonight, I'm tired." Ray went silent, and I felt his hand slip off my knee.

"Whatever, Cass. Go home." I could feel the disappointment in the car.

"Please don't be like that, Ray."

He didn't respond, just stared ahead. All that was on my mind was Brody and how he lit me up like the fourth of July when he had kissed me tonight.

The first thing I did when I got home was put the kettle on, then pulled all the blinds closed across the back of the house. It was cold tonight, and the glass from the windows and sliding doors was just magnifying that temperature. I needed to build a fire and was happy I had brought in lots of wood before leaving this morning. Missy came running and greeted me in the kitchen, meowing like crazy.

"You must be hungry, huh, Missy? Sorry, I'm so late," I said, giving her a pet and grabbing a can of food out of the fridge for her. She danced happily around my feet as I put food in her bowl and set it down on the floor. I watched as she attacked it viciously.

Once I had everything done, I looked at the clock. It was only nine-thirty but felt so much later. I grabbed my laptop from the table and curled up in my favorite chair with a blanket while I waited for the fire to finally start to heat the house. I needed to get some words out tonight, and I hoped it would provide a distraction from the thoughts running through my mind. The store had been so busy today, and it had taken away from my plans of writing. However, there hadn't been any quiet time, which wasn't a bad thing, but with my deadline looming,

I needed to get this book written. I was starting to feel super stressed which wasn't going to help matters.

The TV droned on in the background while I reread the few paragraphs I had written the night before. I needed to get into my characters heads. I was just about to start writing when my cell pinged with a message. I had a good mind not to answer it, I needed no more distractions, but when it went off again, then again, I felt I had no choice. I had the alarm company who monitored the store set to message my cell phone if anything was wrong and three messages in a quick period had me wondering. I grabbed it from the table.

As soon as I saw that the first two messages were from Ray, annoyance set in, but when I saw the third message, a surge of heat ran through my body as my heart began to pump a little harder. A soft smile formed on my lips as I reread the message from Brody. I was going to reply, but instead, I dialed Brody's number, a funny flutter floating in my stomach.

The phone rang a couple of times, and I was just about to end the call when I heard him pick up. As soon as his deep voice came over the phone, I felt it travel straight to my center.

"Hey, Sexy."

"Is now a good time?" I said, ignoring his comment.

"Anytime is a good time to talk with you."

"What are you doing here, Brody?" I had to cut right to the point, I couldn't risk getting hurt again.

"I got a transfer." the line went quiet. "I went to see you down in Greyfield, but you moved."

"I didn't have much of a choice. Things got pretty tough for me."

The line was quiet for a moment. "Because of me?"

How was I supposed to answer that? Indirectly, it had been because of him, but I didn't want to put all the blame on him. Lying in bed for months on end with no will to do anything had also put me in that position. I thought for a moment.

"It was many reasons, not just you."

"I see, I'm sorry, Cass." The line went silent again. I could hear him breathing so I knew he was still there. "So, did you ask that ass why he lied to me? He never did answer me."

"Brody, Ray is a good man. I'm sure he was just protecting me. Don't read into it, okay?" I didn't know why I was defending Ray's actions, I wanted to know as well why he had lied to Brody.

"Sort of hard for me not to. I didn't like the smug look on his face tonight."

I did my best to ignore that comment. I wasn't about to get into it with him. "When did you move into town?"

"Last Saturday. I'm living at the fire station until I can find a place, so until then, this will be my new home."

"What do you mean you're living at the station? Don't you have anywhere to stay?"

"No, not yet, the transfer was really fast. Of course, with Christmas coming, it's near fucking impossible to get hold of anyone who owns any rental property up here, they're all on vacation."

"Brody, you can't live at the fire station until after Christmas."

"Sure, I can, what else do you suggest I do, Cass?"

I took a deep breath. It probably wasn't the best idea I had ever come up with, and I was positive Ray wouldn't like it, but I would deal with him later. I wasn't letting Brody spend Christmas in the firehouse alone, no matter how angry I was with him. I swallowed hard.

"I have a spare room, Brody, you could always stay here with me."

"You sure about that, Cass?"

"Yes, you can stay here as long as there isn't any funny stuff like this afternoon. You can't do those things, Brody."

"Do what?" he feigned innocence.

"You know exactly what I'm talking about." I heard his deep chuckle come over the phone.

"What about Ray?" he asked in a mocking tone.

"Just let me deal with him, Brody. You can come by the store on Monday, or you can just come here after the work day is done. I close at five."

The line went quiet again, and when he spoke his voice took on a somber tone. "When did you start working at the bookstore, Cass?

I looked down at the flashing cursor on the screen. I didn't know what to tell him. I wasn't sure I wanted to tell him the truth just yet or just make something up.

"Cass?"

I cleared my throat, "When I moved here. I just needed something to occupy my time," I lied. He didn't need to know my writing career had plummeted, and I was the owner. "Listen, I'll tell you more when I see you. I'll have a spare key made for you this weekend I'll have it with me on Monday, in case you want to move in while I am at work."

"Alright, I'll see you then. Good night, Cass."

"Night."

I hung up the phone and sat staring at my blinking cursor. My phone pinged with a message. I looked down at my phone, another message from Ray.

Ray: I see you're still up, I'm coming over.

I rolled my eyes, I just wanted to be alone. I was so tempted to text Ray and let him know Brody would be staying with me. That news would be enough to make him stay home, but I knew he would be pissed, and truthfully, I feared how he would react if we were alone. I didn't want to spend the night in an argument. Brody was a friend, and even though I was angry with him for what he did in the past, I needed to move past it and get on with my life. I'd explain everything to Ray in time. I felt confident that he would understand after he got over his anger. I typed out a text to him and went and unlocked the front door.

Chapter Nine

Cass

Ray collapsed on top of me, breathing hard, his sweaty body sticking to mine. He gripped the top of the condom, pulling himself from me and headed toward the bathroom. "Just going to shower, I'll be back." I watched as he left the room. When I heard the shower running, I let out the breath I was holding and ran my hand over my face.

Ray had been able to sense how distraught I was, he had come right out and asked me tonight when he arrived. I didn't have the heart to tell him what was on my mind, and I felt awful. Since I had seen and spoken to Brody, he was all that had been occupying my thoughts.

I listened to the water run and rolled onto my back,

staring at the ceiling, thinking back to this afternoon. Brody's words replayed in my mind—*Am I too late, Cass? Please tell me you're not dating this guy? He's got to be twenty years older than you. I mean, is he even able to get it up?*

Sure, Ray was older than me by twenty years or so. He was divorced with a daughter about my age. Our relationship certainly wasn't what I would have thought I would have found myself in after Jackson. He was a rather rough man, but he was a hard worker, and he treated me well. However, the more I thought about our relationship, the more I felt something was missing. I didn't feel it could go much further than where we were right now.

The longer I lay there thinking about my relationship with Ray, the more Brody started to enter my mind. I grabbed my phone off the bedside table and opened my chat, debating on whether or not to send a message to Brody. Just as I was about to start typing, I heard the shower shut off. I went to put the phone back on the table when the screen lit up with a message.

Brody: It was good to talk to you, and to see you. Sleep well, see you on Monday.

I smiled to myself and reread his message. I tapped the side of my phone and bit my bottom lip as I thought about how to respond, then I quickly began typing.

Cass: Would you like to come for dinner tomorrow night?

As soon as I hit send, I felt a ball of nerves in my stomach start to quiver, and it felt like hours had passed while waiting for his response.

Brody: Absolutely

Cass: I'll message you tomorrow with the time, you should already know the address.

I shut my phone off and set it beside me. The bathroom door opened, the light went off, and I could see Ray's silhouette as he made his way back over to the bed. I had silently been hoping he would shower and head home as usual so I could be alone, but instead, he crawled in beside me.

"Are you sure everything's alright? You seem so distant tonight."

Normally, I would cuddle up to him afterward, the only time I got any real intimacy from him, but not tonight. Tonight, I wasn't in the mood.

"No, I'm fine," I said, rolling away from him and onto my side.

I felt the bed move and his body press against mine as he put his arm under my head, his other arm around my waist, pulling me into him.

"Are you sure? You can talk to me if something is bothering you."

"Yep, I'm sure" I could feel the tears start to burn my eyes. "Just tired."

He pulled me closer to him and pulled the covers up

around us. I closed my eyes tightly and sighed. I didn't want more physical closeness than what we'd already had.

"Maybe you need to take some time off?"

"Take time off from what? I can't take time off from the store, Ray, I have no employees. Taking time off would mean closing."

"I don't mean from the store, Cass. You're stressed. I meant from writing this book. I just don't understand your need to write it. You're working yourself to the bone."

A tear rolled out the corner of my eye. I didn't want to hear this again even though I feared he was right. Writing part of this anthology meant I would be working a full day at the store and long nights with probably very little sleep. But I didn't care, all I wanted was support, but he would never understand. The relaunch could mean so much for me. He didn't understand this was where my passion truly was because he hadn't known me then. I didn't respond to his comments. Ray had voiced his thoughts to me more than once on this topic, and I was tired of hearing it. Instead, I changed the subject.

"What are your plans for tomorrow?"

"I have a bunch of errands to run, and I'm having dinner at my daughter's place tomorrow night. You should come. You should meet her."

"No, it's good, I'm going to relax at home." The last thing I wanted to do was meet his daughter. I already knew that she didn't approve of our relationship. It was odd enough for me dating someone who was so much older, and since I wasn't sure what direction we were going, I figured it was best not to get involved with his family at this point.

"Good, you need it," he said, kissing my neck. "Now, get some rest."

It wasn't long before he was finally asleep, snoring loudly, finally relaxing his grip on me. Despite how tired I was, my mind wouldn't shut off, and lying here beside him tonight just felt so wrong when my mind was on someone else. I glanced at the clock. It was two, I couldn't lay here anymore. I slipped out of bed, grabbed my phone, and left the bedroom, shutting the door softly, careful not to wake him.

I placed two logs on the fire, grabbed some water, and curled up on the couch. I closed my eyes, my mind instantly wandering back to this afternoon. I couldn't get that kiss out of my mind. What was bothering me, even more, was every time I closed my eyes tonight while Ray and I were having sex, it was Brody I saw.

Chapter Ten

Cass

The smell of chicken and roasted potatoes permeated the house. My stomach let out a loud growl as I opened the oven door, warm heat blasting my face. I pulled the rack out of the oven that held the roasting pan and quickly basted the chicken, giving the potatoes a quick stir. Shutting the oven door, I looked around the kitchen. The coffee cake sat cooling on the rack on the counter. I was surprised it had turned out, it had been so long since I made one.

This was the first real home-cooked meal I'd had in over two weeks. I had been trying to make something healthy on Sundays, so I could have leftovers for a couple of days, but that hadn't been happening lately. It wasn't easy to cook for one, and it had become my new normal to eat something out of a can or box. I found by the end of the night, I was so tired and didn't feel like putting forth the effort. I turned to check the table—it was set for two, a small candle burning in the center, a bottle of wine chilling in the fridge.

My stomach felt uneasy as I checked the clock. It was a little after five, Brody was due to arrive at five thirty. I had purposely chosen that time because I knew Ray would be well on his way to his daughter's, and he wouldn't be back until after eleven or possibly even the morning. I had been planning to tell him about Brody moving in with me this morning, but I wasn't even sure how to bring up the subject without starting a fight.

I went to clean up the mess I had made so far when my phone pinged with an email. As soon as I looked at the incoming message, my stomach started to feel queasy. It was enough having the nerves of being alone with Brody, I didn't need anything else to help. It was one of the authors working on the anthology, wondering if I was okay with the editing date. She had emailed me earlier this morning, but with Ray stomping around, I hadn't answered her.

I was still so behind and barely had a couple chapters down, and I wasn't proud of any of them. I had never had this much trouble writing in the past, the stories used to just flow. I knew it was all due to the lack of support I felt from Ray—I had never not been supported before. I found it beyond frustrating not to be able to share something like this with him. Jackson had been so supportive, he always wanted me to run everything by him as I wrote, and now, without that, I guess my confidence was waning.

I took a deep breath and hit reply, typing out the response I was hoping to avoid. I had to let her know there was a possibility I would need a small extension. I knew it wasn't what she wanted to hear, but hell, at the rate I was going, she would be lucky to have my part of the anthology by the end of January which meant they would have to push out the release date. I didn't want to let this affect me though, I wanted to start out on the right foot.

The knock on the front door caused me to drop my phone on the counter. Missy had torn off down the hall. I hit send and walked over. Taking a deep breath to calm my nerves, I slowly let it out before I pulled the door open. There he stood, his jacket flung over his arm. He wore jeans and a white cable knit sweater that hugged him tight in all the right places. He looked more built than I remembered, now that I got a good look at him. He was holding a bouquet of red and white carnations, and when he spoke, his voice went right to my center.

"Evening, Cass." He held the flowers out for me to take.

"Hi." I was unsure of my voice, so I stepped off to the side to let him in, taking the bouquet from his hand.

"Smells good, Cass. I've missed your meals." He gave me one of his sexy half smiles.

"I hope you brought your appetite. I made your favorite dessert too."

"You know it."

I shut the door behind him and went to the kitchen to put the flowers in a vase while Brody took his boots off, my hand shaking the whole way.

Slowly, he wandered into the kitchen, looking around the room before he sat down on a stool at the island. In the few seconds he had already been there, I felt completely comfortable and totally at peace.

"What can I get you to drink?"

"I'll just have water right now, please."

I poured two glasses of water and set his down in front of him, my eyes meeting his. I could feel the tension in the air.

"So, how have you been? How was your day?"

"Quiet. First quiet day I've had in a while. Yours?

"It was good, busy," I smiled.

Suddenly, Missy let out a loud meow and jumped up on the stool beside Brody.

"Who is this?" Brody asked, reaching out and petting Missy behind the ears. She rubbed against his hand, purring loudly.

"That's Missy, we kind of adopted one another."

"Is that so? Well, hello, Missy."

"Yep, she has lived with me for a couple years. I found her outside the front door two years ago at Christmas time. I wasn't going to let her in, but the weather was so bad, she probably would have died out there. She was just a baby, I think someone may have dropped her off. So, I brought her in, gave her some food, and from then on, we became best friends.

"She's a lucky cat to have picked your door."

"Tell me about it," I laughed. The room got quiet again as our eyes met. I watched his eyes travel my body which made me feel uncomfortable, knowing he was checking me out.

"So, are you still writing?" Brody had been super supportive of my career after Jackson died, always wanting to help, but unlike Jackson, he had never seen what I truly went through while trying to write because, by that time, my career had already started to die. He never saw the endless hours I'd spend staying awake while trying to meet a deadline or how stressed I'd become over a new release.

"I am," I lied. Well, it wasn't really a lie, it was more like the half truth. "Just before you got here, I had a couple emails back and forth with another author about an anthology I'm working on." As soon as the words fell out of my mouth, I instantly regretted them. I didn't want him to know the truth. "I'm also working on a pretty complex storyline for another book, and I had to ask my editor for a bit of an extension. Good thing she's flexible,"

I laughed, hiding my eyes from him, taking a sip of my water. That was a total lie.

I could feel his eyes following me as I walked to the fridge to grab the bag of carrots. He knew I was lying, I knew it. I had never been a good liar and didn't know who I thought I was kidding—myself or him.

"Well, I'm sure whatever it is, it will be great. Care to share with me what it's about? It will be like old times, I always loved listening to your ideas."

I closed my eyes, afraid he would ask. Good thing my back was to him, so he couldn't see the sheer panic on my face—I had literally nothing to share with him. I cleared my throat and started peeling the carrots. Just as I was about to start to make something up, the oven timer beeped.

"Time to baste the chicken again."

Grabbing the hot mitts, I opened the oven door and quickly basted the chicken. As soon as I was done, I placed it back in the oven, closed the door, and turned to throw the mitts on the counter across from me, but instead, I came face to chest with Brody. He placed both hands on each of my arms.

"Can I help with anything?"

I looked up, studying his eyes. I was afraid to look for too long, fearful he would be able to see everything I was hiding. I instantly became lost in them. It had been so long since I had looked closely into those gentle blue eyes, and I had missed them.

"You look tired, Cass, maybe you should take a load off. Give yourself a break."

I let out a restricted laugh, I could feel myself starting to crumble. "A break? I wish I could take a break, Brody, a whole lot of breaks, but I can't. I just have a lot on my plate here, things you don't understand."

"What do you mean?" His voice was soft as he ran his hands down my arms, pulled the oven mitts from my hands, and placed them on the counter, his hands returning to mine.

I shook my head and tried to pull out of his grasp to turn away, but he gripped my arms and kept me facing him. As soon as our eyes met this time, I could feel my lips start to quiver. He felt so safe to me, and if his persistence kept up, I would be a puddle in his arms, and I didn't want that tonight. I just wanted to spend time with him, getting reacquainted. Our gaze was so intense. I felt his hands loosen their grip, and I pulled away from his comforting touch. I turned away and went back to peeling the carrots, but I could still feel the heat from Brody's body standing behind me. It was comforting, and instantly, I started to calm down. He reached around me, his chest pushing into my back as he grabbed my hand that held the peeler, his touch sending shock waves through me.

"Cass, let me do this, go sit down, take a load off," he whispered in my ear. Chills ran through my body as his breath danced over my skin.

I stilled, knowing I needed to let him take over even for only a few minutes. I needed to get hold of myself. I stood rigid for what felt like minutes, fighting what I really wanted—his lips on mine while he held me close. When he put his strong hand on my shoulder, I leaned back into him, letting my body rest against his hard chest. I was so confused. I wanted to tell him the truth, I didn't like lying to him, it wasn't the way I wanted to start off. His return was proving to be more than I could handle. I was just about to confess when I felt him pull the peeler from my hand.

"Cass, please go relax."

"I'll pour us some wine," I said as I released the peeler and grabbed the edge of the counter to steady myself.

"That sounds like a good idea."

I walked over to the fridge, glancing back over my shoulder. He reached behind his head and pulled his sweater off. He was wearing a white t-shirt underneath, and I couldn't help but watch as his muscles flexed beneath his shirt. I loved how the muscles in his forearms and hands flexed with every stroke as he peeled the carrots. I started to wonder what it would be like to have those hands on my body once again, how good they would feel doing forbidden things to me. What it would feel like to have his lips kiss me all over my body, sucking my nipples into his mouth.

"Are you getting us wine?"

The sound of his voice pulled me away from those thoughts, and I pulled the wine bottle out of the fridge and put another in. I poured us each a glass and took a sip before handing Brody his glass.

"Thanks. Now, go sit down."

I took a seat at the table and sipped the cool liquid.

"So, when are these upcoming books set to release? I take it you're working away on them; how much do you have left to do?" Brody asked, stopping to take a sip of wine.

Why couldn't he just let this go?

"I just started the one and maybe got a couple of paragraphs done today. It's the other one I'm worried about," I lied. "I just sit and stare at the screen. You could never imagine the power of a blank page with a blinking cursor." That part wasn't a lie.

He was quiet for a moment. "Well, can I help you with it?"

I laughed at his question, this felt just like old times. "Sadly, you can't. I wish you could."

"I remember Jackson would tell me how you would bump ideas off him. Surely, if he could do it, I could help you with that too. I have a pretty damn good imagination."

I got quiet, remembering the last idea I had bumped off Jackson—it had been so long ago, but it had ended in a marathon of sex against the kitchen wall. The realization of what he had just said shocked me.

"He used to tell you about that?" As the words passed my lips, I could hear the shock in my own voice, and I swallowed hard.

"Why? What's wrong with that, Cass? He just said when you used to get stuck, you would talk to him about it. So, I thought maybe I could help you, at least listen to your idea, maybe you just need to talk it through out loud."

I let out the breath I had been holding with a nervous laugh. Thank God he had his back turned toward me and couldn't see the light flush on my cheeks.

"Excuse me for a second, I just need to use the washroom." I got up from my chair and headed down the hall. I walked into the bathroom and shut the door, looking at myself in the mirror.

"Why are you lying to him, Cass?" I asked my reflection. Just be honest with him, he should know the truth. I stood and studied my reflection, completely disappointed with myself when I heard the phone ring. I quickly flushed the toilet and made my way back out into the kitchen.

The evening had gone well after I returned from the bathroom. We ate dinner, enjoyed dessert and coffee together in front of the TV, Brody had even built a fire. We talked endlessly, catching up. I was disappointed when he had to leave, and after saying goodnight, I shut and locked the front door. I watched through the small window in my front door as he walked to the truck. I couldn't help but check out his ass in those tight jeans one more time before he left. The sexual tension in the air had dissipated once he had left the house.

I'd had a hard time concentrating all evening. It was the quiet moments when the words seemed to get lost, my mind had traveled to the kiss at the store. I was constantly wondering what he was thinking when I would catch his eyes wandering to my lips. I wanted more of that and to feel what it would be like if I were trapped underneath him, wrapped in his strong arms again. I watched as he climbed into his truck and drove out of my driveway.

I ran my index finger over my lower lip, remembering that kiss. Once Brody's truck was completely out of sight, I shut off all the outside lights and the one in the front window, then pulled the blackout shades down across the front window, so it looked as if I were asleep. I knew Ray would be home soon, and I didn't want to give him any indication I was still awake. I went down to the bedroom and did the same thing, pulling the curtain across the window.

After I had changed, I made my way out to the kitchen and started to clean. I had finished loading the dishwasher and had put the last pot in the dishpan when my phone pinged with a message. I dried my hands and grabbed my phone.

RAY: ALMOST HOME, YOU UP FOR A VISIT?

I contemplated answering but thought it was best if I didn't. Instead, I shut my phone off, placed it on its charger, shut off everything else, and went to my bedroom. I had to be up early to get to work, and for some reason, I had a bad feeling telling Ray that Brody had been here for dinner and would be moving in here with me tomorrow wasn't going to go over well, but he needed to know.

<h1 style="text-align:center">Chapter Eleven</h1>

Cass

I barely had time to stop since the store opened. Donations for the book drive were steadily coming in, and even some tourists were purchasing books for the charity. When the store had finally quieted down, I grabbed a coffee and another box and started filling up some of the empty spots on the shelves. When I was finished, I took out my laptop and sat down behind the counter. I needed to get some writing done, and while I waited for the next group of shoppers, I couldn't think of a better time. I was working away when someone caught my eye. Brody walked by the front window and up to the door, the little bell ringing to let me know someone had come in.

"Hey! I brought you lunch." Brody strolled in, holding up a small brown bag. There was no mistaking the smell of what that small bag contained.

"That isn't what I think it is, is it?" I inhaled deeply again, the smell of pho soup making my mouth water.

"Sure is! I remember how much you love the stuff. I was just on my way back into town and passed this little restaurant. You'll probably have to warm it up a bit."

I walked over, took the bag from him, and headed into the small kitchen. I couldn't wait, my stomach was already grumbling.

"I haven't had this in ages." I had practically lived on this stuff after Jackson had died, it was the only thing that was easy on my stomach. It was my favorite comfort food, and since Brody had loved the stuff just as much as I did, he never minded going.

I popped the container into the microwave and entered in the time when I heard the bell ring out front. I poked my head around the corner to see who it was.

"Hey, May, I'll be right out, just warming up some soup."

"Take your time, dear, I'm just going to browse."

"Okay. There are some new releases in the Romance section I think you'll love," I called back.

"Wonderful, dear, thanks."

Going back to the kitchen, I removed the soup from the microwave, stirring it and placing it back in to heat it some more. "Thanks for the soup, Brody. You must have read my mind because I forgot to pack a lunch this morning."

"No problem, Cass, figured you might be hungry. You look a little on the lean side to me."

"Yeah well, most days, I don't have much time to eat anything."

"You should make time."

I grabbed my purse from the floor, ignoring Brody's comment. I dug through it, looking for my spare key. When I couldn't find it, I thought for a second and remembered I had left it sitting on the counter in the kitchen.

"Dammit, I forgot the key.'"

"That's okay, Cass, I can just swing by after you get home. I have a bunch of things to get done, anyway."

"No, no, here, take my key. I normally get home around seven-thirty. If you're not going to be home, make sure you leave the back door open so I can get in." I removed the key from my key ring and held it out. Our eyes locked as his fingers grazed my hand as he took the key, and I swallowed hard. "Don't let Missy out, she doesn't go outside anymore."

"No problem, Cass, I can do that."

The back door opened, and I heard Ray's heavy footsteps coming toward the kitchen. I closed my eyes and blew out a breath. I hadn't had a chance to speak with him this morning, and this was certainly not how I wanted him to find out.

He came around the corner, and as soon as he saw Brody, the smile fell from his lips. His gaze darkened as he walked over, leaned in, and met my lips, but my eyes never left Brody's.

"How's your day going?"

I met Ray's eyes and gave a forced smiled when he pulled away.

"Good, been busy. I'm tired."

"Well, if you weren't staying up all hours of the night wasting your time working on some silly story, you wouldn't be so tired."

Brody cleared his throat to say something, but I gave him a look, silencing him before dropping my eyes to the ground. I was trying to get used to Ray's reactions and thoughts about my writing. If we were going to be together, I needed to get used to the fact he wasn't going to be supportive, no matter what, and nothing would ever change his mind. The microwave beeped again, and I removed the soup and set it on the counter.

"What's that?" Ray questioned.

"Soup, Brody brought me lunch," I smiled and winked in Brody's direction. Brody smiled back.

Out of the corner of my eye, I caught Ray glaring at Brody. "Well isn't that nice of him?" Ray huffed.

"Cass, I have to run, thanks for the key, I'll see you

tonight. Enjoy your lunch," he winked and headed back out front, the little bells jingling as he left. I couldn't help but smile to myself as I watched him walk out of the kitchen.,

"What the fuck was he doing here, Cass? What key?" Ray demanded, looking after him. I closed my eyes at the sound of the anger in his voice.

"Calm down, he just needs a place to stay, he just moved here. I won't have him stay at the fire station over the holidays."

"Don't tell me to calm down. Where is he staying, Cass?"

I bit my bottom lip. I didn't think Ray was a jealous guy, but maybe I had misjudged.

"Cass? I asked you a question."

"He's staying at my place. I do have a spare room sitting empty."

"The fuck he is!" Ray answered, raising his voice.

"Keep your voice down, May is outside."

"I don't give a fuck who is out in the store. Bottom line, you're not going to share your place with him."

This was not how I expected the conversation to go.

"Well, I am, Ray, he's a friend, and that is exactly what I plan to do." I had to put a stop to this before Ray continued to cause a scene. The last thing I wanted was to argue with him in front of my customers. "Now, what did you stop in for?" I glared at him.

"I came to see if you wanted to come by tonight for a couple of drinks, but I think I've already got my answer."

I was so behind on my deadline, I needed to get work done, but judging from how he had reacted about Brody, I didn't dare tell him no. "I will come by for one drink. I'll see you around seven."

Ray stormed out the back-door minutes later. I was upset, I didn't like him telling me what I could or couldn't do. Once I gathered myself, I took my soup back out front. May was sitting in the armchair in the front of the store, reading through the beginning of a new Danielle Steel book.

"Oh dear, I'm trying to remember if I have read this one," she mumbled to herself.

"I'm pretty sure you haven't read that one," I called over to her.

"Well, dear, she has so many, it's so hard to keep up."

"It's brand new, May, it just came out this week," I said, giggling to myself. While May continued to look at the pile of books she had set on the small table beside her, I took a sip of my hot soup and started writing again.

I arrived at Ray's a little after six-thirty. I wanted to get this drink over with, so I could get home. It had been an extremely busy day. I still had work to do tonight, and I wanted to make sure that Brody felt at home and comfortable.

Ray had been so angry when he had left the store, and since I hadn't heard from him the rest of the afternoon, I wasn't sure what mood I was going to find him in.

By seven thirty, he was pouring me a third drink even though I told him I didn't want anymore. He was onto his fifth or sixth, I had lost count. While he was busy, I stepped into the bathroom and pulled out my cell phone. I typed a quick text to Brody, letting him know I would be home in the next hour. Almost instantly my phone pinged with a message.

Brody: Thanks for letting me know. make sure you come hungry, I'm making dinner

I smiled and shoved the phone back into my pocket, flushed the toilet, and headed back out into the living room. I hated it when Ray drank heavily, especially when he was angry. He came up behind me as soon as I stepped into the living room and wrapped his arm around me, holding my drink out in front of me. I took the drink from his hand and went to set it down, but instead, he wrapped his arm around my waist and started kissing the side of my neck.

"Put the drink down," he purred. I set the drink on

the table and went to turn around to face him, but he held me where I was, continuing to kiss and suck on my neck. I closed my eyes, trying to ignore the smell of alcohol on his breath. I was having a hard time feeling anything but violated.

His hand ran down the flat of my stomach to the button on my jeans. With one hand, he opened the button and shoved his large hand inside my panties.

"Ray, please." I grabbed his wrist to stop him.

"Please what? Why are you stopping me? Is it so wrong I want to fuck you that I want to taste this sweet pussy?" He breathed into my ear and sucked my earlobe into his mouth. He slid his hand deeper into my pants, pulling me tighter against him so I could feel his erection digging into me.

"Ray, please stop. I don't want to do this while you're drunk." I could sense the shake in my voice as I pulled at his wrist, the smell of beer on his breath becoming nauseating.

"Cass, what the fuck! It's because he's here, isn't it? He comes strolling into town, and suddenly, you aren't interested in me at all."

"Don't be ridiculous, it has nothing to do with him. You know how I feel about your drinking like this, and I've already told you once tonight, I'm not in the mood." He let me go and pulled his hand from my pants. I quickly fastened the button on my jeans and took a step away from him. I was shaking as I walked over to the door, grabbing my jacket and purse.

"I'm going to go, Ray."

"Sure go, I know you want to get home to him," he spit out, taking another swig of his beer.

"You're drunk, Ray. Don't bother talking to me until you've sobered up." I pulled the door open and quickened my pace to my car. I was afraid he might try to follow me.

Once I was inside, I locked the doors, sitting there fighting my tears. I was so upset, I could taste the bile in my throat. I started the engine and pulled out of Ray's driveway. I didn't have far to drive, so I pulled over to the side of the road and sat there for five minutes, trying to calm down before I went home. If Ray was going to continue treating me like this, I would have to take some time and figure out how much further I wanted this relationship to go.

Chapter Twelve

Cass

I walked through the laundry room, my head hung low. I had calmed myself down enough to be able to come home. I hung my coat and purse on the hook behind the door and stepped into the kitchen. I looked up and stopped. The lights were dimmed, candles lit on the dining room and living room tables, and soft Christmas music floated through the air. The table was set for two, full of serving dishes, and a bottle of wine was sitting in my wine chiller on the counter. A fire was lit, the wood stove doors were open, the screen mounted on it.

I walked in a little further, running my hand along the clean kitchen counters. I went over to the table, lifting the lid off one of the serving dishes, the smell of home-cooked food making my tummy grumble.

This should be what I should have come home to, not a drunken brute of a man who was turning out to be someone I feared I didn't know as well as I once thought. I lifted a lid on another dish and took a deep breath, smelling the hot food.

"Welcome home." I dropped the lid back down on the dish and straightened up. I looked over my shoulder and saw Brody standing in the hallway door, looking amazing as ever. He wore light blue jeans, ripped in a couple of spots on the legs and his black t-shirt hugged his muscles in all the right spots.

"What's all this?"

"I told you I was making dinner. I hope you're hungry."

I looked back at the table and back at Brody. With everything that happened at Ray's after I had sent the text to Brody tonight, I forgot Brody was making dinner.

"This is wonderful..." A sob escaped my throat, and I squeezed the bridge of my nose.

"Cass?"

I held my hand up toward him, signaling him not to come any closer, but it did no good. I soon felt the heat from his body behind me, and I held it together until he placed his hands on my upper arms.

"Cass, what is it?"

I shook my head but couldn't fight back the tears anymore. I turned and wrapped my arms around his neck, letting his scent invade me as I buried my face in his neck. Ray had been so horrible and had scared me so much, I just couldn't take it. It was more than just that though. Having Brody back, all those unsaid feelings and thoughts running through my mind was harder on me than I thought it was going to be. Everything was fine until he came back, I thought all the want I had for him was gone. I hoped I would be able to hold it together, but from the second I saw him, he was all I wanted. When he wrapped his arms around me, I totally lost it, hard sobs racking my body.

"Did he hurt you?"

I shook my head no. Brody would kill him if he found out that yes, he had, in fact, hurt me.

"Are you sure?" He pulled me in tighter, and I could feel myself relax in the safety of his arms.

"I'm sure," I mumbled into his chest.

He held me, letting me cry until I had totally calmed down, his strong arms keeping me safe. "Alright, well how about we eat?" he finally whispered.

As soon as dinner was over, we were just about to make our way over to the couch when Brody's cell phone rang. He pulled his phone from his front pocket and glanced at the screen.

"I've got to take this, it's work."

I watched as he walked back into his bedroom for a couple minutes, and the next thing I knew, he was running to the door.

"I hate to do this Cass, but I've got to go. Are you okay to clean everything up?"

"Of course. Just be careful."

"Always am."

I watched him go, praying for his safe return.

Chapter Thirteen

CASS

The last couple of days had been a blur. I was still angry with Ray, so it was probably better that he hadn't bothered coming around. After Brody had left the other night, I had cleaned the kitchen and gone to bed, but sleep was nowhere to be found. When my head hit the pillow, the tears started. It wasn't that Ray had hurt me, it was more he'd scared me. I was a mess, and it had taken me a much longer time to calm down than I thought it would. I was glad Brody had been called to work because it would have only been a matter of time before I would have told him everything and probably would have spent the night crying in his arms, instead of into my pillow.

I was so thankful the day was over. I was about halfway up my driveway when suddenly, the house lit up like a Christmas tree, white lights running along the edge of the peaked roof and around the windows. That was when I spotted Brody's truck pulled in and under the trees that lined the driveway. The call must have been serious, this was the first time he had been home since he left the other night. Judging from all of this, he had been home for a while. At least long enough to put up Christmas lights. I pulled my car into the garage and headed into the house.

The smell of roast beef crashed into me the second I walked through the door, and my stomach let out a huge growl. Again, another day had gone by where I had nothing to eat but cookies. I dropped my purse onto the dryer and hung up my coat. Walking around the corner, I was greeted by Brody's ass in tight jeans, bent over the open oven door. When he stood up, I couldn't help taking in his bare back, muscles flexing as he picked up the pot on the stove and drained it in the sink. I leaned against the door frame, watching him work around the kitchen. He looked so much stronger and much more built than I remembered.

"What do we have here?" I said smiling.

"Cass! I hope you don't mind, I figured you might like to come home to dinner, so I got us a roast, cooked some potatoes, and I was just about to steam some broccoli."

"Do you always cook half naked?" I said, my eyes traveling down his bare chest to his tight abs. I could feel the heat in my face as my eyes skimmed over his body—he was in top physical shape.

"Yeah, I'm sorry, it got a little hot in here with the fire going and the oven. Come in, sit down, let me pour you some wine."

I walked in and took a seat at the breakfast bar, watching Brody as he poured two glasses of wine.

"Thanks, but you better be careful, I could get used to this," I said, grabbing the glass from his hand and taking a sip, letting the cold liquid roll down my throat.

"What? Me half-naked in your kitchen?" he chuckled. "I hope you do," he winked. "Are you feeling better than you were the other night? Did you get a chance to talk with Ray?"

"Don't be silly, everything is fine," I lied, looking away from him. "Here, I'll grab the plates." I jumped off the stool and gathered some plates and cutlery.

"You sure about that?"

"Yep, we talked everything over, we're good," I nodded. I don't know why I was lying to him, but I didn't want to give Brody the wrong impression of Ray by telling him the truth about what had happened.

"I see you put up Christmas lights." I dropped the plates onto the table, trying to change the subject.

"I did, I hope you don't mind, this place needed a little Christmas pick-me-up."

"Not at all, Brody, they look nice."

We sat in the living room after dinner, eating dessert while relaxing by the fire. When we were finished, I took our empty plates and set them both on the living room coffee table. Grabbing the remote, I started searching through the channels for a movie. It seriously felt like nothing had changed between us in all the time we had been apart. Everything about being around Brody had such an ease and comfort to it, something I wasn't used to anymore. I grabbed the blanket off the back of the couch and draped it over my legs, leaning back into the couch.

"You cold?"

"A little." Brody's arm was resting across the back of the couch right behind me, his hand draped over, touching my shoulder.

"Why don't you snuggle up here? You remember, I'm like a human furnace."

I felt a little uncomfortable when my arm brushed against Brody's side, but it wasn't like we had never cuddled before. As I relaxed against him, I couldn't help but breathe in his scent, the scent of him mixed with his cologne smelled so good. He pulled me into him and rested his arm around me. I seemed to be very aware of his every move, and it would have been okay if I didn't have a nagging feeling in the pit of my stomach. I took a sip of my wine, trying to ignore the voice in the back of my head that was wondering why Brody had come back after so many years.

I had just started to relax against him when he spoke, "So what made you start working at the bookstore?"

I looked down at my half-filled glass of wine before I answered the question—he wasn't going to like the answer, considering I lied to him the other night. I was sure he already knew that though. Brody had never wanted me to give up on my writing, and after Jackson died, he always pushed me to do my best. I took another sip of wine and a deep breath before I answered him.

"I don't just work there Brody."

"What do you mean?"

"Well, I own it. I'm the sole owner and sole employee." My eyes finally met his.

"How can you do both?"

"Well, I have to be there, anyway, so there really isn't any point to hire someone and have a payroll to worry about—I'm barely turning a profit. That's why for the book drive I have been looking for volunteers."

"That's not what I meant, Cass. How can you write full-time and work full-time?"

I took another sip of wine, not looking in his direction. He knew the truth, I wasn't fooling anyone, and he also knew the hours I used to spend writing which back then had left little to no time for anything else.

"Cass? What about your writing?"

"It's a long story, Brody." I took in a deep breath and closed my eyes, I couldn't look at him.

"So, tell me."

"I'm trying hard to start up again. I had the option to write a part for a romance anthology with a few author friends of mine, so I took it. The other book I told you about, I made up."

"So, you lied to me the other night." He went silent, grabbing his wine.

"I didn't want you to be disappointed in me."

"I'm more disappointed you wouldn't tell me the truth. At least you're starting again I guess. That's what really matters. I hope Ray is supportive of the idea. It's not my place, but I didn't like his comment to you the other day."

"He's not really that supportive." My finger ran around the rim of my wine glass. "He doesn't understand, he was raised to be a worker, and he doesn't look at it as work. He thinks it's just a waste of time, and I should focus all my time on the store."

"I see. Well, I'm going to try not to make any comments on that, but I'm happy for you. You were a great writer."

"How would you know?"

A light blush rose to his cheeks. "I may or may not have read a couple of your books."

I smiled a little at his admission and took a sip of wine. "You read my books?"

"Let's just forget about that, but in the meantime, if you need help with your writing, I was serious when I said you can bounce ideas off me. Remember, Jackson would never have wanted you to quit."

I took a drink, the mention of Jackson's name making me a bit uncomfortable. I looked at the picture that sat on the table beside Brody, his eyes following mine.

"I miss him, Cass. A lot. It's weird being here. The last time I was here, I was with him on that fishing trip, just a couple of months before the fire. Not much has changed, you've kept it pretty much the same." He turned his attention back to me after looking around the room.

"That's not true, a lot has changed, Brody."

Brody continued to look around the room, and I watched him. He hadn't changed. For the first time since he had returned, I really looked at him. He was still as handsome as he ever was—Those blue eyes set against his dark hair, his chiseled jaw set tight with a couple days worth of growth. I couldn't help take in his features as he looked around the room, his eyes falling back to the photo. When our eyes met, I remembered Jackson's words the night he died.

"I don't want you to spend the rest of your life alone if ever I don't come home. I want you to go on and meet someone, get remarried, have kids, and live your life and never give up."

I hadn't done a great job following his wishes. Here I was in a relationship with a man who was twenty years older than me. I knew he was past the stage of wanting children, he had made that very clear, and I doubted if he wanted to get remarried. So, here I was in a relationship with very little hope or want of it moving forward, and I had totally given up on everything I had worked hard for. There had been so many days in the last three years that had been a struggle to even get up out of bed.

For whatever reason, it could have been the memory I just had or the fact I was sitting here with the first man I had slept with after Jackson had died, but I could feel the tension between us. Perhaps it was the three bottles of wine we had consumed or all the unsaid things that lay there, hidden between us, but whatever it was, for me to be able to move on and start over with Brody, the air needed to be cleared.

We sat in complete silence, studying one another. At one point, I almost thought Brody was going to kiss me, but he didn't. When I couldn't take the tension anymore, I blurted out the first thing that came to my mind.

"Brody, seriously, why did you come back?" I knew exactly how this question sounded, but it had been gnawing at me since Josie had sent me that text, letting me know he was looking for me.

"I had to see you."

"What for, Brody? You think you can just come walking back into my life just to leave me again?"

"I suppose that's fair."

"You suppose that's fair? What the hell, Brody?"

"Cass, don't get angry."

"Don't get angry? What did you expect, I would welcome you with open arms, and I wasn't ever going to say anything? Fuck, Brody."

"You sort of did. That kiss Cass, I can't get it out of my head," he said, taking my hand in his.

I ripped my hand away. He'd struck a chord with that comment. I knew I had made a mistake by not pushing him away, but fuck, the man could kiss, it had been a nice fucking mistake. Still, I stood up and headed to the kitchen. I didn't want this to turn into an argument, things were getting too heated. We'd had too much to drink, and nothing good could come out of two people arguing under the influence. I ought to know, it was a recurring situation with Ray.

"I feel like shit, I didn't plan on leaving you, Cass. Please, just let me explain."

I crossed my arms and stood glaring at him. "I'm waiting."

"That night, after you pushed me away, I felt this tremendous amount of guilt for acting on my feelings for you. The way I felt about you, I'd never felt that way about anyone. It scared me. I was supposed to be there to look after you. I promised Jackson I would look out for you, take care of you. Instead, for months, all I wanted to do was get you fucking naked and make you moan and writhe underneath me. Then when it happened, I couldn't get enough of you, I wanted to consume every fucking inch of you every time I was with you."

I felt myself blush at his admission. I wanted to stop him right there, but I continued to listen.

"But when you stopped me that night, for whatever reason, I realized maybe my feelings may have gotten out of control, and maybe you weren't as ready and wanting as I was. So, I did what I thought was right. I had to find some way to get you out of my head because I'm pretty sure that wasn't what he meant by 'take care of you.' So, as much as it hurt me to leave you, I figured it was the best and only solution for the both of us. It wasn't supposed to be for three years, Cass, just until I got things under control. Only, I soon found out I was wrong by leaving and these feelings weren't going to go away quickly, if ever.

I thought about you and wanted you more and more as time passed."

My anger took over as soon as he stopped talking. I was angry he left, angry at myself that I stopped him that night, and angry at him because he hadn't ignored me and taken me again that night like I had really wanted him to, like he should have.

"So, instead of facing your feelings, you left when I needed you the most, Brody. It wasn't enough that I had just lost Jackson, you had to walk out of my life too, just like that, without even a fucking goodbye."

"I left you a letter."

"Yes, you left me a letter. A letter that almost fucking killed me after I read it. I struggled and struggled to make sense of why you left, and to be honest, I haven't been able to. And after all this time, I'm still not able to because your reason isn't good enough. We're fucking adults, Brody, all you needed to do was talk to me." I could feel the tears burning my eyes, but there was no way I was going to cry in front of him.

"I never said it was a good enough reason, Cass. I was a coward."

"Yeah, that's exactly what I would call it. You promised me, and you promised him, Brody. I know you did because I fucking heard it when I got to the hospital that day." I slammed my fist down on the counter.

"Yes, you're right, I promised him. I fucked up, I

know that. I know what I did was wrong. I live with the memory of that promise every damn day. He's disappointed, I know it, I feel it."

The room was silent as I fought with myself about what direction to go next. I wanted to say I forgave him, and no matter how much time had passed, I still had feelings for him—but I couldn't. I couldn't let those words pass my lips, not yet, I wasn't sure I was ready. My heart was pounding, and I could hear my pulse whooshing in my ears, and I felt dizzy. Instead of saying what my heart wanted me to, my anger came back in full force.

"After you left, I fucking lost everything. I didn't leave my bed for almost four fucking months, my mom had to come stay with me, I was a mess. I couldn't write, my career died, and after that happened, everything that was left spiraled out of control. I came close to losing the house. Luckily, I was able to sell it and got a bit of money, but it only made things worse. I had to leave the home I loved, Brody. I couldn't eat, I couldn't sleep, and those nightmares, they returned and just kept getting worse. Suddenly, it wasn't just Jackson who had died in that fire, Brody, it was you too. It was like I lost you both all over again. You not only fucked up with him, Brody, but you fucked up with me too."

I was so angry and hurt, I had to turn away from him. I had been holding onto all of that since the night he had walked down the front steps of my house. The tension in my shoulders and back was unbearable, my hands balled so tight into fists, my nails were biting into my flesh.

"And just so you know, I had feelings for you too, Brody. I wanted you just as bad that night, and every night before, just as much as you wanted me, maybe even more. And no matter how right or wrong it may have been, those feelings were and still are very real. You weren't the only one who was scared. That's why I stopped you, I wanted to tell you."

"Why didn't you say anything?"

"Why didn't you?" I shot back. I kept my back to him, a couple tears escaping—I couldn't stop them now. Suddenly, I could feel the heat from his body behind me, his hands on my shoulders, his breath on my neck.

"I'm sorry, I shouldn't have left you, and I'll never forgive myself for what you went through. I was selfish." He squeezed my shoulders in his strong hands. "All this time apart has done is show me I need you in my life, Cass. But now, you're with him. Tell me what I can do to get you back. I'll do whatever it takes!" He wrapped his hand around my waist, pulling me into his chest.

"I don't know, Brody. I needed you in so many ways— to comfort me, to make me laugh, make me forget, make me feel loved." Those were the things I still needed, the things I never received from Ray.

"I know you did, I wanted you so fucking bad, I still do. It just took me this long to accept it's okay, Cass, okay to want you and to have you." He kissed the back of my neck, lightly grazing his lips over my skin, sending a warm chill through my body.

"Brody, don't do this," I whispered. As soon as I blinked, I felt more tears fall over the rim of my eyes.

"I can't fight how I feel for you anymore. You've never left my heart or my mind, that tells me something. As soon as I saw you, it was like I never left, the same feelings stirred in my gut as they did that night."

I closed my eyes, resting my hand on his. "Brody, I can't do this. I'm going to go to bed," I choked out, swallowing the large lump in my throat. All it would take was him to kiss me, really kiss me like he had done the other day in the store, and I would melt into his arms. He didn't move, just held onto me, his breath at my ear.

"Don't push me away, Cass. That kiss was real, I felt it, and I know you felt it too. Tell me you're happy with him, that he treats you well, and I'll bow out, I'll leave you be. But if you can't tell me that, don't deny it, don't deny us, don't deny me, and give us the chance we both deserve," he whispered.

I pulled out of his embrace, keeping my back to him and took a step away.

"I need to go bed." It had taken everything I had not to cry, but my body betrayed me as I started to shake while I was still standing there, sobs filling my throat. I wanted that chance as well, I couldn't deny that.

He reached for me, wrapping his arm around my waist and pulled me into his chest. He placed his hand on my cheek, his thumb brushing away the one tear. He looked me in the eye and slowly leaned in and brushed his lips against mine until he was kissing me deeply. I could feel my body start to melt against him but stopped and pulled at his hand, forcing it away from my body.

"Brody, please, I can't do this now I'm going to go to bed."

I saw the hurt in his eyes and felt his hand slip away from my body. I ran down the hall, and as soon as I was in the safety of my bedroom with the door closed, I leaned up against the door and slid to the floor. With my face in my hands, I let out a deep sob. There was no doubt I loved the feel of his lips on mine and his hands on me, my body pressed into his. I was meant to be there. Soon the tears stopped, and when I heard the creak in the hallway, I got up from the floor, got changed, and crawled into bed where the tears started all over again.

Brody

Maybe this was a mistake, I thought as I was left standing in the living room alone. I had watched her make a beeline for her bedroom, her shoulders shaking more and more with every step she took.

I hadn't even made it a full week yet, and I had already made her cry. I felt horrible. I took a deep breath and blew it out through my mouth, looking in the direction of her bedroom, debating if I should go down there. Instead, the mess of dirty dishes on the counter caught my attention. They weren't going to clean themselves, and I didn't want Cass to be up half the night or wake up to the mess in the morning.

I wandered over, listening to faint cries coming from down the hall and started to load things into the dishwasher after putting the remainder of food away in the fridge. I even set aside a container for Cass to take for lunch tomorrow. She wasn't looking after herself very well, and I'd be damned if that was going to continue.

Once I had everything put away, I threw two more logs on the fire and sat on the couch, listening to her murmured cries, each sob a knife to my heart. I debated what to do. Walking away was the easy part, I had done it, and it got me nowhere. I was determined not to do that this time even if she was crying because of me. I planned to tough it out.

After a while, the crying stopped, and I got up from the couch and shut the light off. I was going to go to bed, but instead, I passed my room and went to the end of the hall. I wanted to talk to her. I stopped outside her closed bedroom door and could tell she was still awake because a faint light was falling under her doorway. I pressed my ear to the door, hearing her soft voice.

"Why should I give him a chance Josie... because of a kiss, are you kidding me? Sure, it was the best kiss I think I've ever had, but come on Josie, that isn't enough..."

I kept my ear pressed to the door, a smile coming to my lips. I wanted to hear more, but she had gone quiet suddenly. I was just about to pull away when I heard her speak again, getting a little louder this time.

"You can't ask me that... okay fine, from what I remember, the sex was great too, but that isn't enough to base a start of a relationship on... I thought we were great together as well, and I have missed him... no, I'm still with Ray."

Listening to her admission, I hung my head and wondered what the fuck I was really doing here. I should have walked the other way when she told me she was seeing Ray, but the part of me that was completely in love with her wouldn't allow it. The jealous part of me, well, that just made me want to fight for her and pray it turned out in my favor. Still, I was angry with myself, but I couldn't fucking help it. I knew she wasn't happy with him—the look on her face had said it all when he had kissed her in front of me the other day—she just needed to see it.

I leaned my forehead on her door and closed my eyes, listening hard, but the room had gone quiet again. I clenched my fists tight. I had to get out of here, I couldn't take it. I walked back down the hall to the kitchen, grabbed my keys off the counter, and walked out the door. I just needed some time to clear my head.

Chapter Fourteen

I pulled the truck up outside of the only bar in town and shut off the engine. I probably shouldn't have driven down here after all I had had to drink tonight but fuck it. If I needed, I would take a cab back home. I needed to figure out what I was going to do. I had deserved everything she said to me, there was no doubt.

Carl's Place was the local bar. It was dark, dingy, dirty, and smelled of stale beer. The few patrons inside turned and looked at me as I entered and approached the bar. It didn't surprise me, small town and all. Tourists probably never ventured in here, they would just stay at their hotel. I ignored the stares, ordered myself a beer, and took a seat at the bar. I was just about done my first one and had ordered another when I heard a gruff voice behind me.

"What the fuck you doing in here? This place is for locals only."

I didn't turn around, I didn't want any trouble. I just wanted to have a couple of beers and be on my way.

"Hey! I asked you a question!"

I felt a hand shove me from behind. I turned around to see Ray staring at me.

"Look, I don't want any trouble, I just came in to have a couple of drinks, alright?"

"Well, that makes two of us, you don't want trouble, and I don't want you shacking up with the chick I'm fucking. But one of us doesn't seem to care about that!" He staggered toward me. I didn't need him getting up in my face, talking about Cass as if she were just another notch on his belt. She meant more to me than that.

"You see, Brody, since you got back into town, the bitch won't even kiss me, doesn't seem interested at all, and that's pissed me the fuck off."

"Well, Ray," I could feel my blood start to pump, "maybe she just isn't interested."

"Nope, that's not it. I tried to get into those tight pants the other night, but she started crying and begging me to stop. Now, the only reason why she would do that, I can think of, is because of you." He poked me hard in the chest.

I clenched my jaw; this guy was asking for it, and he was going to get it if he didn't back the fuck up. I took another swig of my beer.

"Well, if she isn't interested, maybe you should just leave her alone, Ray." The few people who were in the bar were starting to take notice of us.

"Fuck you!" Ray shouted into my face. That caught the attention of a few more people in the bar and the bartender.

I was about ready to pummel the guy. My patience was being tested. Ray turned to take a step away from me.

"Let me ask you, why didn't you tell me where she was that day?"

"What fucking business was it of yours, come in asking after my woman?"

"She's a friend, and I asked you a question."

"I'll tell you a little secret, no one in this town comes asking me about anybody, especially about the woman I'm seeing. Now, I'm not going to tell you again, leave her alone."

"Or what? What the fuck you going to do? She doesn't want you, Ray, so you may as well give up now!"

"Get. The. Fuck. Out."

Two men approached from the back of the bar and grabbed hold of Ray. "Ray, let's get you out of here, man, before you do something you're going to regret."

"Fuck you, too!" He pulled out of their grips. "This

asshole is living with that fucking broad I'm banging. I don't like it, and I'm going to put an end to it."

"You're drunk, Ray, let's go, you need to sleep this off," the one guy said. Ray glared at me, his pupils dilated, his breathing rapid, his body completely tense. "You're not putting an end to anything, come on Ray, let's go, man." Ray finally turned and headed toward the door.

I took another swig of my beer, then decided to provoke the old ass some more. What can I say, I can be an asshole as well?

"You're banging her, that's a fucking joke," I laughed. "I seriously doubt you can even get it up any more, old man, and if you can, what, you last all of four minutes?" I shouted. "Does she even get turned on by you? Cause I know she had no problem getting turned on when I kissed her the other day. Right. Under. Your. Nose."

Ray stopped in his tracks and turned. "What did you say?" Ray said through clenched teeth, his fists tight, forming two balls.

"You hard of hearing too, old man? I think you fucking heard me. I fucking kissed her."

Ray charged forward, heading straight toward me, taking a swing. I ducked and came up under him punching him in the gut. Ray buckled over, coughing and spitting.

"Unless you can talk about her with respect, I don't want to hear you say another fucking word," I spat.

I thought Ray was going to walk away, but he took a cheap shot, punching me. As his fist connected with my mouth, I felt a searing pain and could taste the rusty metallic taste of blood.

"Get him out of here, I've had enough of his behavior," I heard the bartender yell from behind me, directed toward Ray and the two men. For a small woman, she sure had lungs on her. I watched as the two men took Ray outside. I got up off the floor and took the towel the bartender offered me to clean the blood off my split lip.

"You alright?" she asked.

"I'm fine," I said sitting back down.

"You shouldn't provoke him, he's got a temper."

I wiped my mouth with the towel, and the next thing I knew the door opened and Ray came flying back inside. He staggered over to me, grabbing me by the jacket collar and pulled me off the stool I had been sitting on. As soon as he let me go, I hauled off and punched him in the gut again, forcing him to let me go and buckle over in pain.

"Get your fucking hands off of me, and if you know what is good for you, you'll leave her the fuck alone."

"That's it, Ray, get out of here, or I'm calling the cops."

I wasn't waiting around either. I punched Ray one more time and walked out of the bar, leaving him curled on the floor while I headed for my truck. I was in no shape to drive even the short distance to the fire department, never mind all the way back to the house. So, I quickly opened the browser on my phone and looked up the local cab company.

Cass

The house was quiet, but the wind howled outside. I was curled under the duvet, Missy sleeping at my side, curled into a tight ball. I was trying to get warm when I saw lights come up the driveway. I glanced at the clock, it was well after midnight. I had just gotten back into bed after getting a glass of water and noticed Brody was gone. It must have been him, at least I hoped it was, I didn't want to get up again to answer the door at this hour. God forbid it was Ray in one of his drunken stupors. I listened hard and heard a key in the front door, then I saw the lights back away. I sat up, climbed out of bed, and parted the blinds so I could look out the window, watching a cab leaving the driveway. I frowned, Brody's truck was gone.

Continuing to listen, I heard a creak in the hallway, followed by a drawer opening in the other room. A few minutes later, the TV went on in the living room. I rolled over, staring at the doorway. I wanted to go to him. I had been so cold toward him earlier, but I couldn't help it, I needed to get everything out of my system. Now as I lay here thinking of him, I wanted everything to be over. I just wanted to be held by him, to be wrapped in his arms and let him know he was forgiven.

I shut my eyes, praying those thoughts would go away and sleep would eventually come, but it didn't. A loud bang caused me to jump. I crawled out of bed, my heart in my throat and walked quickly down the hall. Brody stood in front of the fireplace, wearing nothing but boxers as he placed a couple more logs into the fire. My eyes skimmed over his muscular back. I couldn't help but check out his ass wrapped snuggly in his boxers. I stayed hidden in the shadows and watched him. As he turned back toward the couch, my eyes continued wandering his body. In the dim light and without his shirt, his muscular chest was better than I remembered. My eyes trailed down to his tight eight-pack, his boxers hanging low enough, I could see his deeply carved vee. Ray couldn't hold a candle to Brody's muscular physique, and my mouth watered at the sight.

He climbed back onto the couch and threw the blanket back over him, turning his attention back to the news. I stood there in the darkness, watching him. He placed his hands behind his head, and I took in the slow rise and fall of his chest. Suddenly, he cleared his throat, and his deep voice seemed loud in the quiet room.

"Why don't you come out here and keep me company,

instead of hiding in the dark watching me." He kept his attention on the TV, not looking at me until I slowly stepped out of the darkness. He still didn't look my way, just pulled the blanket back for me to crawl in beside him.

I felt my heart speed up at the thought of lying with him, the warmth of his body warming me. My legs were shaky as I took a couple steps forward, holding onto the wall for support.

"Have you slept?"

I shook my head as I walked toward him. I watched his eyes as they trailed the length of my t-shirt clad body. There was no mistaking the look in his eyes even in the dim light.

"My God! What happened to you?" I said as soon as my eyes caught his swollen split lip.

"It's not a big deal, just come here," he said, lifting the blanket for me to crawl under.

Instead of crawling in beside him, I went to the kitchen and got a cool, wet cloth. Walking back over, I sat beside him, pressing it to his swollen lip.

"What happened?"

"I had a bit of an altercation with a fist, really it's not a big deal."

"What happened, Brody?"

"I was defending someone's honor."

"Seriously, Brody? You got into a fight? Where were you?" Brody winced as I pressed the cloth to his lip.

"I went to the local bar, I needed to clear my head, don't worry about it."

He pulled the cloth from my hand and threw it down on the floor and lifted the blanket for me to crawl under. I looked at him, trying to read what was behind his eyes.

"Well, are you going to lay with me or not?"

I let out a breath and shook my head. I stood up and went back down the hall toward my room. "Goodnight, Brody."

"Come on, Cass, just come lay with me."

"I said, Goodnight!" I slammed my door hard and crawled back into bed. I knew Ray spent most evenings at the local bar and would almost put money on it that he was the one Brody had been in a fight with. I also knew resting my body beside Brody wouldn't end well, the desire that had been radiating through his eyes told me he would have completely consumed me. I turned my back to the door, pulled the blankets up to my neck, and closed my eyes, waiting for sleep to come.

Chapter Fifteen

When I woke in the morning, Brody had already left for work. I was happy I didn't have to see him this morning. I was cranky, irritated, and tired, having floated in and out of sleep all night, finally staying asleep after four. I had another long day ahead of me, and I was already exhausted and running late which only made me crankier. Just as I was about to run out the back door, a note on the counter caught my eye. *Don't forget your lunch.* That was all that was scrawled on the yellow sticky note in Brody's hand-writing—my eyes stung with tears. Opening the fridge, I pulled out the container and headed out the door.

All the way to the store, I beat myself up for not even

giving Brody the chance to explain what had happened last night. I didn't know for a fact it was Ray he had fought with, and I probably would have slept a hell of a lot better if I had just crawled in beside him, curled up against him, and let him explain

I pulled up behind the shop and checked my watch. I normally started an hour before the store opened, but this morning, I only had about fifteen minutes. As I approached the back door and slid my key into the lock, the door was abruptly opened, causing me to jump. Ray stood inside, looking out at me.

"Cass, there you are. I was worried when I stopped across the street for coffee this morning and saw you weren't here, so I came over and got things started for you. I was just about to come up to the house and make sure you were okay." Ray didn't open the garage until ten on Saturdays, so he normally came in to give me a hand. I didn't expect to see him this morning though since we hadn't spoken in a couple of days.

"Thanks, Ray," I said, pushing past him, throwing my purse and coat on the hook inside the door.

"Cass, I want to apologize for my behavior the other night. I was wrong."

"It's fine, don't worry about it." I walked past him into the kitchen and threw my lunch in the fridge.

"Cass, are you sick? You look pale."

"I'm fine, just had a bad night." I headed to the front

of the store, checking over everything. I didn't want to get into it with him right now. I just wanted to focus on the task at hand and pretend everything was fine, and nothing was bothering me.

"Have you eaten?" he asked, concern in his voice.

"No, I haven't, I didn't have time."

"How about I go over and grab you a coffee and some cookies before I leave?"

"Whatever you want, Ray," I huffed as I straightened up a couple of shelves I hadn't had time to do last night. I was never short with him. He had helped me so much, and I was truly grateful, but honestly, I wasn't in any mood this morning to be nice to anyone. If I'd had the option, I would have just called in sick.

Ray stood watching me, a worried expression on his face. I tried to ignore it, but he was getting on my nerves.

"Don't stand there and stare at me Ray. I said I'm fine." I avoided looking at the concern on his face and bit my lip to try to stop the flow of tears I felt coming on. I was exhausted and emotional, and it would only be a matter of time before the tears started to fly if he didn't leave me alone.

"Cass, what is it?" he asked, his deep voice turning soft and muted.

The books I was looking at started to blur as tears filled my eyes—exactly what I didn't want. My chest felt like it was going to explode as the sobs poured from me.

"How much time do you have," I sobbed. I went to run past him into the back, out of sight from the storefront, but he grabbed hold of me and pulled me into his arms. As soon as I hit his chest, I was done, I couldn't hold it back anymore.

His hands smoothed my hair as I cried into him, letting go of everything I had been holding. The loss of Jackson, Brody returning, the pressure Ray was putting on me—it all just poured out. When I didn't calm down right away, he pulled me into the back, away from the front of the store where people were starting to gather outside.

"Cass, you have to calm down, sweetie, it's time to open. How about I take you for a drink after work, we can talk then?"

"I'm a mess, Ray. Look at me, I can't face customers like this."

"It's okay, I have about a half hour I can spare. Why don't you sneak out back, go and get a coffee, and I'll open up for you?" He gave me a squeeze as he let me go.

"Thanks, Ray, I owe you."

"Well, one day when I'm not feeling well, you can come and do a couple of brake jobs and change some oil for me." I giggled through my tears at his suggestion. "Go on, go grab your coffee."

I grabbed my jacket, heading out the back door as Ray headed to the front and welcomed my customers. I walked across the street and into the coffee shop. I only had a half hour to calm myself down, and I planned to do it quietly in a corner of the coffee shop with a cup of coffee and a bagel.

"Hey Cass!" Melanie said from behind the counter. "What can I get for you?"

"Can I get a coffee and a toasted bagel, please?"

"Sure, love. Everything okay? You look a little down this morning," she asked while getting my bagel ready to toast.

"Yep, just had a long night."

I watched as she poured the coffee into the cup and wrapped my bagel, handing them both to me. I made my way to the back corner, sat down and started to eat. I was about halfway through my bagel when the bell jingled above the door. I wasn't going to look but curiosity got the best of me, and I turned to see Brody enter with two other men. At first, he didn't notice me, but as he was waiting for the other men to place their orders, he turned toward me, a smile coming to his lips. He excused himself and approached my table. Taking his coat off, he sat down across from me.

"Why aren't you working?"

"Ray is over there, I was running late this morning. He stopped in to make sure everything was open for me."

"Wow! A true hero," Brody commented sarcastically.

"Brody, don't do this."

"Yeah, well, I need to talk to you about your saint over there."

I glanced at my watch, it was almost nine and I did have to get back over to the shop. "Alright. Not now. How about tonight?"

"Fine, what time will you be home? Seven?"

"A little later than that, I'm having dinner with Ray."

I could see the annoyance written all over Brody's face. "Whatever, if you need me, call me."

I frowned. "Brody, why are you behaving this way?"

"Cass, without letting me explain, just promise me if you need me, you'll call."

"Alright, fine. I have to go." I stood up and balled up the wrapper from my bagel, threw it in the trash, and grabbed my cup from the table. "Have a good day, Brody."

"You too. Cass."

Chapter Sixteen

Cass

I locked the day's deposit in the safe and went to shut off and clean the coffee maker when Ray came through the back door.

"Hey, Cass, hope your day was good."

"It was, I hit record sales today. At least something went right," I smiled as he followed me into the little kitchen.

"How about yours?" I questioned. I grabbed the carafe and dumped the coffee down the sink and filled it with hot water and soap.

"It was okay. I got word from my supplier the parts I ordered are in the warehouse, but they can't get the shipment to me until after the fifteenth of January. I need them for the tenth which means I'm going to have to make my way down to pick them up."

"That will be like a two-week trip! You won't be here for the book drive, and right now, you're the only help I have aside from Brody." I could feel the tension creeping into my shoulders yet again.

"No, I'll wait until after Christmas, no worries. I'll be here," he said, massaging my shoulders and neck gently.

"Thanks, I really need you to be here for that, it means so much to me."

"I know it does, you don't need to worry. I thought we would go grab a bite, then I could take and help you pick out a tree. I noticed the other day you still didn't have one up."

"To be honest, I don't think I am going to get one this year, Ray. I am not much into celebrating Christmas anymore."

"But you said you wanted to get one."

"I know what I said, but I've changed my mind, is that not okay?"

I could tell Ray was annoyed with me, and I didn't blame him, I was annoyed with myself. "Did you want to go for dinner or just want to go home?"

As I did the final rinse on the coffee pot, I could hear Brody's comments from this morning in the back of my mind, *Call if you need anything*. At first, I wondered why

Brody would have said that, but now that I could hear the irritation in Ray's voice and could feel him studying me, I started to understand.

"No, I'm up for dinner, I'm starving."

I followed Ray over to the little Italian restaurant down the road. Once seated, Ray poured us both a glass of wine from the bottle he had ordered as we waited for our food to arrive.

"So, you want to tell me what got you so upset this morning. I have a feeling it has something to do with Brody."

I took a sip of wine. "Yes, it does."

Ray nodded, grabbing a breadstick from the basket on the center of the table.

"I know you don't like him, Ray, but you need to understand the history we have."

"Then why don't you tell me."

I took a sip of wine to clear my throat before I started.

"You see, after Jackson died, Brody was my rock. He spent a lot of time helping me around the house, having dinner with me, keeping me sane—basically pushing me to continue to live. One day, we started looking at one another differently, and things between us started to change. I was starting to become attracted to him in a way that kind of scared me. Shortly, things got serious between us, and neither of us was sure where it was going to go. We started arguing.

"Then one afternoon, there was a bad fire in town, and they reported some firefighters missing. I guess that was when I really noticed how I truly felt. I tried to get hold of him, but he didn't answer. Finally, after a few hours, he showed up at my door. I was a mess, I thought I'd lost him as well. I was pretty much devastated. He came in, and things started to get intimate between us. I ended up stopping him.

"I already knew I felt things I had never felt before, not even with Jackson, and before they went any further, I wanted to be able to tell him how I felt. He wouldn't talk to me, assumed I stopped him because I didn't want anything else to happen and went home. The next morning, he was gone. He left me on Christmas Eve, so it kind of ruined this holiday for me."

Ray looked at me with sympathy filled eyes. "What do you mean he was gone?"

"Gone, he had taken his stuff and left. He didn't call, but I found a note from him a day or so later. The only people he had notified were his landlord and the guys at the fire department. That's when things got bad for me. I had no desire to do anything after he left. It was like I had lost Jackson all over again. I lost everything, Ray. Everything—my career, my home, and my best friend." I stopped talking as the waitress dropped our food off at our table.

"I'm going to admit, Cass, the points aren't stacking up in his favor after hearing this."

"I know, but I feel you need to know our history."

"I appreciate that. So, now he's here and staying with you," Ray said, passing me the pepper.

"Yes. We had a long talk last night, and it just brought up some old memories and feelings. I was pretty upset when I went to bed."

"Tell me he didn't hurt you?"

"God, no."

"Good, I don't want to have to teach him another lesson."

"What's that supposed to mean?"

"What does what mean?"

"Don't do this, Ray."

"Don't do what?"

"Ray, this whole situation has brought up lots of feelings, feelings I had buried away. There were a lot of things said on both our parts last night, things that needed to be said for us to both move on and get past everything that's happened. I guess it was just a lot of pent-up emotion we each needed to get out."

"And that's what had you so upset this morning?"

I took another sip of wine and took a bite of food. "Yes and no."

"Care to elaborate?"

"I feel the need to forgive him, but I'm not sure I can."

I looked up from my plate. Ray sat there with his wine in hand, his eyes meeting mine. He said nothing, just sat there studying me, taking me in.

"You don't have to forgive him. Unless... do you still have feelings for him, Cass?"

I swirled my fork around my plate, thinking about the question. After five minutes of not answering him, I finally cleared my throat.

"I'm not sure I know the answer to that," I lied.

"It's easy. Either you do, or you don't."

"It's not that easy, Ray. He really hurt me when he left, but at the same time, he was all I had."

"I understand that, but I don't think it would be bothering you this bad if you didn't have some sort of feelings for him."

"I'll always have some sort of feelings for him, that isn't going to change. He was with me during a time I couldn't possibly take care of myself. I lost my husband at twenty-six years old. It wasn't supposed to be that way."

"I fucking knew it!" he said, slamming his fist on the table, causing the dishes to jump. People glanced over at us.

I looked around the restaurant, taking in the stares from many people who knew the both of us, then I put my hand over his.

"Calm down, Ray. Please, you're creating a scene."

"So, let me ask you, when he kissed you the other day,

it brought up some of those feelings, didn't it?"

"I don't know what you are talking about, Ray. He didn't kiss me," I answered, swallowing hard.

He was watching me like a hawk, taking in my every move like he was ready to pounce. He had a look in his eyes, and I feared he knew I was lying to him. I took a sip of wine, trying to pretend I didn't notice.

"I take it he told you why he left."

I nodded, taking another mouthful of wine. "He said he needed to sort out his feelings about us."

"I see. What conclusion did he come to?"

I felt the food rise into my throat. I really wish he hadn't of asked me that question, so I tried to pretend I hadn't heard him.

"Cass, I asked you a question."

"You did, I'm sorry I didn't hear you."

"What conclusion did he come to since he's been gone?"

I grabbed my glass of wine and drank down the last couple mouthfuls.

"He made a mistake."

"I see. Well, I'm sorry, Cass, but I know he made a huge mistake," Ray said, taking hold of my hand.

"Why is that?"

"Well, if I were him, that's how I would feel, especially seeing now you are in a committed relationship with someone else, and he can't have you, he's too late."

I pulled my hand away. I clearly didn't feel the same way about him as he did about me. His words had made me feel extremely uncomfortable. I turned my attention back to my meal.

"Listen, why don't you come to my place tonight? I think it will do you good to have some space away from him right now, get things right in your head. We'll go grab the trees, then you can help me decorate mine, we'll have wine, watch a movie or two, cuddle up together by the fire, just be together and relax."

I studied his expression for a moment, thinking about his offer. Sure, it sounded great, but I didn't need anything else to complicate matters right now. I didn't know how I felt about him or our relationship anymore.

"Or I can always come by your place and spend the night there? Make sure Brody understands you're not available for whatever it is he thinks he's going to get. Plus, to be honest, I fear for your safety around him."

I couldn't believe my ears. "What is that supposed to mean?"

"Oh, he didn't tell you?"

"Tell me what?"

"He came into Carl's last night, drunk, provoked an argument with me, and we got in a fight. He was down there spreading shit about you, Cass. Talking about you in filthy ways, how he wanted to fuck you and wanted me to stay away from you. I dealt with him."

"So, you're the one who split his lip?"

"He's lucky that's all I split after the things he said. He ran off like a pussy afterward. I want to make sure you're safe, Cass," he said, rubbing my hand with his.

I wasn't sure I believed what he was saying. Brody wouldn't talk about me in a bad way, I knew better than that.

"Ray, I'm good, really. I'm going to go home, alone. I just need a good night's sleep and a few days to get myself out of the funk I'm in."

"Pushing me away again. So maybe your feelings for him are greater than you say?"

"I'm not pushing you away. Don't put words in my mouth."

"Don't worry, it's understandable, he's younger and not a bad-looking guy. You don't have to tell me if you have feelings for him or not Cass, I can tell. The good guy always gets shit on."

"Don't be that way."

"Be what way? Clearly, you are siding with him. Don't worry, I'm not going anywhere, I'll still be a pain in your ass."

I felt horrible. I could tell from the look on his face he was crushed or possibly pretending to be. "I'm sorry. All of this, honestly, couldn't have come at a worse time."

"It's fine."

The tension that fell between us during the remainder

of the meal was almost unbearable. I turned down dessert, and even though he insisted he pay the bill, I took this one. I didn't want anything looming over my head with him.

"Ray, I don't want there to be tension between us. I don't want things to change. I just need some time to get myself sorted out," I said as he opened my car door.

"They won't change, don't worry. Now, I want you to get home safe before the bad weather hits. I'm going to head over to that lot at the corner and grab myself a small tree," he said, kissing my forehead.

"I feel horrible, Ray."

"Don't, I understand, you need to figure things out. If he hurts you, or if you need me and want to come by, just shoot me a message, and I'll be there. My door is always open." He leaned in and kissed me goodnight, but it didn't feel like goodnight to me, it felt more final. I could even feel his lip quiver against mine.

He pulled my door open and waited for me to get in, then he shut the door. I started the car, and as soon as Ray stepped back onto the sidewalk, I pulled away from the curb. The drive home was quiet, too quiet, so I clicked the radio on, and Christmas music filled the cabin of the car. What a Christmas this was turning out to be. I just wanted to get home, get in my pajamas, curl up on the couch with Missy, a bottle of wine, and relax.

Chapter Seventeen

Cass

When I got home, the driveway was empty. I guess Brody had gotten tired of waiting for me and must have gone out. Once inside, I built a fire—Brody had already brought in lots of wood so I could check that off the list. I quickly threw in a load of laundry, fed the cat, got changed into my favorite pair of sweats and a t-shirt, grabbed my bottle of wine from the fridge, and a glass. I was finally settled under a warm blanket and relaxed as I sunk my body against my fluffy pillow and found a movie on TV. Missy laid curled behind my legs, purring contently as I ran my hand over her soft fur. My laptop sat on the table. I needed to write, but I needed to unwind first. I looked around the small cozy cottage. It wasn't much, but it was now home. The only thing missing was a Christmas tree. I had promised Jackson I would get a tree this year, it didn't really matter I had made the promise to empty air, I felt it was important to keep that promise even if right now, I wanted nothing to do with this holiday.

I leaned my head back and closed my eyes. I was thankful it was Sunday tomorrow. I had so much weighing on my mind, and after everything that was said at dinner tonight, I really wanted to talk to Brody, find out his side of the story. I had a strong feeling Ray was making everything up. I knew Brody could have a temper, but he was never one to provoke a fight, and it didn't sound like him to talk bad about me. I had known him way too long to believe that. But regardless, Ray was my boyfriend, and I felt horrible for leaving him tonight on such a bad note. I grabbed my phone off the table and sent Ray a quick text.

ME: Sorry about tonight. Hopeing you could give me a hand tomorrow? I'd like to get a tree.

Almost instantly a reply came back.

RAY: I know I promised you I would be here for the book drive, but I have to leave town tomorrow. Need those parts for a big repair coming in, it can't wait now. I will text you

*as soon as I get back. Should be gone about a week or two.
Plus, I need time away.*

I felt my heart sink. He had promised, he had promised me he would be here for the fundraiser. Was he doing this to get back at me for treating him the way I had tonight? I swallowed hard and through teary eyes typed my response.

Me: You won't be here for the book drive? You promised

Ray: I should be back the day of. Sorry, Cass, I know this isn't a good time to leave, but I have no choice. You need space, so I'm giving you what you want.

I was pissed at that comment. Sure, I needed space, but I never said I wanted him to leave.

Me: But you said you didn't have to go until after christmas

Ray: Things change, your words. get some rest. I'll come say goodbye before I leave.

I felt a tear roll down my cheek at how cold his comments were. I threw my phone down on the table and turned my attention to the movie. I really didn't want bad feelings between Ray and me, but it seemed there were going to be. I shut my cell phone off, I didn't want to be bothered by him anymore tonight. Pulling the blanket up around my shoulders, I let my body sink into the pillows. A loud knock on the front door caused me to jump.

Frowning, I got uncurled from the warmth of the blanket and headed to the door. "Who is it?" I called.

"It's me, Cass," I heard the familiar deep voice call. I pulled the door open and was faced with a giant evergreen tree.

"What the hell?"

"I got us a Christmas Tree." Brody poked his head through the only open spot there was and smiled his ridiculous smile.

I couldn't help but laugh. "This is going to have to stay outside for the night, I haven't got any idea where the stand is or if I even have it anymore."

"Nope, I got one of those too, Cass. We're bringing this monster in. Now, if you can just grab the base and pull it in, we should be all set."

I bent down and picked up the trunk of the cold tree, and together, we pulled and pushed it through the door. Once inside, we laid the tree down on the floor and shut the door. Brody quickly set up the stand, and we managed to get the monster of a tree set up right in front of the front window. The tree basically covered the big picture window when it was standing up.

"Think you got a big enough tree?" I giggled, looking it over.

"I guess I kind of went overboard, but they only had a couple left, so it was this one or a Charlie Brown tree. There was no way you weren't having a tree this year, Cass."

The smile faded from my lips. The last good Christmas had been before Jackson died. Then after Brody left, I swore off the holiday. The only reason I even had anything in the storefront window was the town made it mandatory. As I stood looking at the tree, my vision started to blur.

Brody stopped pulling the last of the wrap off the tree and looked at me. "What's wrong, Cass?"

"I was just thinking I don't know how many decorations I have anymore. I kept a few, but I haven't unpacked half of the boxes I moved here with. Plus, Christmas just sucks now."

"So, we get a few things, it's no big deal." He dropped the twine on the tree in a pile on the floor, grabbed me, and pulled me into his chest. "It doesn't have to suck anymore."

I wrapped my arms around him, breathing him in. Why did he always have to be so warm and smell so fucking good?

"I know, I say that every year, and every year a new

reason seems to arise, and I want the holiday to go away and never come back again."

"Well, this year it's not going to be that way." He held me, running his hands over my back. "I tried to wait for you tonight, so we could go and pick this tree out together, but you weren't home when I had to leave to pick my truck up from Ray's."

"Don't worry, it's probably better you went on your own." I pulled my body away from him and looked into his eyes, "I would have chosen the Charlie Brown tree, anyway."

Brody smiled and went back to removing the twine from the tree.

"I have some wine. Do you want a glass?" I asked, watching him.

"Absolutely! I'm just going to get changed. Pour me some." Brody headed off down the hall, and I went to the kitchen to grab another glass.

I had just sat down and was waiting for Brody to return when I heard another knock on the front door. Walking over, I pulled the door open to find Ray standing there.

"Hey, sexy," he said, taking me in. He leaned in to kiss me, and I could smell the alcohol on his breath.

"Ray! What are you doing here?"

"I told you I wanted to see you before I left, something wrong with that?"

"No, I just figured you would be leaving tomorrow."

"I am, but early, so I thought I would come by tonight." He stepped inside and looked at the huge tree. "I thought you didn't want a tree, Cass."

"Well, if you read my message, you would have seen I asked you to take me," I huffed. "Brody got it tonight on his way home."

"I see," he said through clenched teeth.

"What's the problem?" I said, reaching to take his hand.

He looked into my eyes but said nothing. He placed his hand in mine and pulled me against him. He was about to lean in and kiss me when something behind me caught his attention. His expression changed instantly.

"Ray? What is it?" He didn't answer, just kept his focus trained on something behind me, his grip getting tighter on me. I turned to see what it was he was looking at. Brody stood in the hallway entrance in nothing but a pair of black sweatpants.

"I see how it is. You wanted to come home tonight so the two of you could play house, is that it?"

"Ray that's enough."

He pushed me to the side and headed straight for Brody.

"Don't be rough with her," Brody stated, squaring himself up against Ray.

"I'll treat her any damn way I want. Let's be clear,

Brody, you're not taking my girl, we discussed this already." His loud booming voice vibrated through the house. He approached Brody, his fists clenched at his side. When he was within reach, Ray threw the first punch, slamming his fist right through the wall behind Brody as he ducked out of the way. I let out a loud scream. I watched as Brody slammed his fist into Ray's stomach, causing Ray to buckle over.

"I'm not taking your girl, Ray," Brody said through clenched teeth. "I won't have to because you're going to drive her away yourself."

Ray stood up and took another shot at Brody, completely missing again, this time throwing his whole body into the little table that sat at the end of the couch. The table went flying over onto its side along with the lamp and my picture of me and Jackson I still hadn't put back into my bedroom. When it hit the floor, the irreplaceable frame shattered into pieces.

"GET OUT!" I screamed at the top of my lungs. Both men stopped in their tracks. Ray looked over at me and saw the tears pouring down my face, then looked down at the broken frame.

"Cass, I'm sorry, I didn't mean to do this."

"Yeah, but you did it. Get out, be on your way, I'll see you in a couple weeks." I opened the door and held it open for him. I'd had enough.

He looked to Brody, then back to me as he got up off

the floor, steadying himself as he walked toward me. He placed his hand on my arm.

"I'm sorry, please, let's just talk."

I couldn't look at him, I kept my eyes on Brody who stood, clenching and unclenching his fists, his jaw tight as he watched every move Ray made, ready to pounce if he laid another hand on me, especially to hurt me.

"Cass, please."

I turned my back to him. "Just go." I mumbled.

He stood there for a couple more minutes, taking me in, probably hoping I would change my mind, and when I didn't, he walked out the front door, head hung low. I slammed the door behind him and locked it. I stood staring down at the remains of the shattered frame Jackson had bought me for a wedding gift, something I could never replace. My favorite picture of us lay on the ground, torn.

I bent down, tears streaming down my face as I picked up all the pieces of the broken frame and placed them into a little bowl that sat on the table.

Brody

I didn't know what to say to her as I stood and watched her carefully lay every broken piece, large or small into that bowl. The bastard had out-and-out attacked me once again, for no reason, and after witnessing him shove her, he was lucky to be walking out of here unharmed. Cass stood there, her hand over her mouth, crying at the mess in front of her. I remembered when Jackson had given her that frame. It had been an early wedding gift for their wedding photo, but she had changed the photo up after he had passed.

I couldn't stand to hear her crying. I knelt behind her and placed my hands on her shoulders, hesitant at first to touch her. I wasn't sure she would even want me near her. She didn't move at first, but then she turned into me, clinging to me like I was the last thing she had in this world. I just held her, letting her cry.

"I'm so sorry."

I pulled back so I could look at her. "What are you sorry for?"

"Him, all of this. Believing the lies that he told me tonight."

"What did he tell you?"

"That you and he got into it down at Carl's because you were provoking him and spewing horrible things about me."

"I see, well that's okay. I'm tough. You, on the other hand, don't seem so tough." In one quick motion, I picked her up and carried her over to the couch. I placed her down in her favorite spot and picked up her wine glass from the table, handing it to her. I then took the blanket she had been rolled in earlier and covered her.

Once she was settled, I went into the kitchen and grabbed the bag of skinny popcorn from the cupboard, poured half the bag into a great big bowl, put the kettle on for tea, and grabbed two mugs from the cupboard.

"Do you think you could make me a tea, please?" I heard her broken, tear-ladened voice call.

"Already on it." It took me a couple of minutes, but I came into the living room carrying a tray with two steaming mugs of tea and a big bowl of popcorn. "Now, I'm going to warn you, I'm a popcorn hog, and you'll have to fight me for it," I winked at her. Finally, I could see the corners of her mouth turn up into a small smile.

"I'll fight you for it." She let out a tiny laugh and pulled her legs up, so she was sitting cross-legged and patted the seat beside her.

Cass

The movie played, and we sat side by side, eating popcorn, neither of us saying anything. I could feel the tension leave my body the longer we watched TV. It helped to know Ray was going away tomorrow. I didn't want to see him for a while after all that had gone on tonight. How dare he come and assume like that, then attack Brody because he was jealous.

When the movie went to a commercial, I cleared my throat, took a sip of tea and asked, "Not that I want to bring this up, but this morning you said you wanted to talk to me about Ray?

"Yes."

"Was it about your split lip?"

"Yes. I can only imagine what he told you."

"What happened, Brody?"

"I'll have you know he confronted me there. He wants me to leave you alone, in case you couldn't have guessed. He's not as nice as you might think."

I was already finding out he wasn't who he had appeared to be. I swallowed hard and took a drink of my tea.

"If I tell you something, you promise not to get upset?"

"Depends on what you're going to tell me." He gave me a small smile.

"He tried to force himself on me the other night when I didn't want him to."

Brody was quiet, his jaw clenching. "Are you okay?"

"I am."

"Why didn't you tell me?"

"I didn't want to upset you, so I just let it be."

"I see, that's why you were crying. Cass, if you are going to pursue anything more with him, please be careful."

"I don't know what I am going to do."

"Well if he keeps this up, I'm probably going to end up in jail, so I hope you figure it out soon."

I turned my attention back to the TV. I went to reach my hand into the bowl of popcorn just as Brody went to reach his hand into the bowl. I looked down when our hands hit, noticing how red and swollen his hand was. I grabbed his hand in mine.

"What is it, Cass?"

"Your hand, it's all swollen, you need ice." I handed Brody the bowl and got up from my spot.

"It's fine, I'm fine," he called after me.

I walked to the freezer and took out ice cubes, putting them into a freezer bag and wrapping it in a cloth. I walked back over, sat back down and took his hand in mine, placing the ice bag on the back of it. I sat his hand on my thigh, holding the ice pack there.

After a bit, I removed the ice and examined his hand, the swelling starting to go down. I ran my fingers gently over the back of his hand and couldn't get the thought out of my mind of what it used to feel like to have his hands on my body, imagining them tracing lines up over my bare legs, to my stomach, and up to my breasts. I couldn't help looking at his strong, broad shoulders and bare chest, thinking about how it would feel to run my hand over him once again.

"What are you thinking about?"

I jumped at the sound of his low voice, and when I looked up at him, he was watching me intently. I swallowed hard.

"Nothing, I was just making sure you were okay." I could feel myself getting warm.

"Do you normally blush when you wonder if people are okay?" He reached over with the other hand and pushed the hair that had fallen into my face behind my ear, his touch sending a jolt of electricity right to my center.

"You're beautiful when you blush," he whispered. Our eyes locked, he slowly inched forward, his eyes running between my eyes and lips. His hand planted on my cheek, he pulled me forward and grazed my lips.

My lips were on fire, and I pulled away.

"It's nothing. I'm not thinking about anything." I jumped up from the couch to take the ice pack to the kitchen. I had to get away from him, I was throbbing. "I think I'm going to turn in," I said from the kitchen.

He got up, bringing the bowl and mugs into the

kitchen. I couldn't help checking him out again, this time noticing the little spray of hair that ran from his belly button down to the outline of his semi-hard cock in his sweats.

"You sure you're okay?" he asked, a smug smirk on his face.

"Yep, I'm good. It's all good."

I watched as he turned and headed down the hall to his room. Then I grabbed the ice pack out of the sink and placed it on the back of my neck. I needed to cool down. I got a cold drink of water and stood in the kitchen, letting the room stop spinning.

Chapter Eighteen

BRODY

I laid in bed, staring at the ceiling, slowly stroking my cock. I was hard as a fucking rock and had been since I had crawled into bed. When I caught her checking me out, I would have paid to hear the thoughts running through that beautiful head of hers. Although I could guess from the light blush that flushed her cheeks exactly what her thoughts had been. I ran my hand up my shaft, precum dripping at the thoughts running through my head. My thoughts so vivid, I could almost see her lying between my legs while her mouth devoured my cock.

I froze as soft light spilled out into the hallway. I watched from the darkness, my hand not moving as she tiptoed by my room, carrying her laptop. I frowned and checked the clock. We had gone to bed almost two hours ago. Why was she still awake?

I squeezed my thick cock, waiting for the throbbing to subside—I was so close and needed to fucking cum. I decided to wait for a bit instead of getting up right away, just in case she was only plugging her computer in, but after ten minutes, I got up, threw on my sweats, and headed out to the main part of the house. I was still worked up, but I wanted to make sure she was okay. I stopped at the end of the hallway, and what I saw before me didn't help matters. I decided to stay tucked away in the safety of the darkness and watched her for a bit. She had only turned on a couple of pot lights in the kitchen. She sat at the breakfast bar on one of the stools, somewhat facing me, wearing a short, pink and black silk bathrobe, bathed in the light from her laptop. As my eyes washed over her body, she reached down and undid the tie on her robe, letting it hang open.

I had to blink a couple of times to make sure I wasn't in the middle of a dream. She was naked underneath. She raised her arms over her head, giving a full stretch, her breasts on display. My mouth watered at the sight. I could feel my cock stiffen again, not that it had had much of a chance to go down much.

I stood there, keeping quiet, watching as she started to type on the keyboard, a sense of peace coming over her face, one I had seen many times. She would type for a bit, stop and place her finger over her lips as she thought about what to type next. Then she laughed to herself and continued to type. I could feel a sneeze coming on and rubbed at my nose to stop it. She stood up and walked over to the fire and threw a couple logs in, turning to face in my direction. Again, I couldn't help checking her out. She went and sat back down, immersing herself back in her book when suddenly, I sneezed. She jumped, looking over in the direction where I was hiding in the dark and scrambled to pull her robe closed. My show had been ruined, betrayed by a dam sneeze. I might as well head out there, she was going to know I was up, anyway. I stepped out of the shadows and walked into the kitchen.

"I hope I didn't wake you," she simply said.

I felt like I was thirteen again, I was so hard. I wasn't embarrassed as her eyes flew to my hardened cock, instead I loved her reaction. She bit her lower lip, her cheeks went pink as her eyes trailed back up my body, finally meeting my eyes before she glanced back to her screen.

"Nope, just needed a drink." I got some water and took a drink, then I walked up behind her. "What are you working on?" I asked, leaning my hands on the counter, one on each side of her, blocking her in. I didn't want her to run from me this time.

She immediately went to shut the laptop, but I

stopped her, grabbing her hands and holding them down underneath mine.

"It's nothing, Brody." She swallowed hard. "Really."

"I'm sure it's not nothing, let me read it," I whispered as I started reading what she had written on the screen. She was in the middle of a sex scene, and damn, I'd be lying if I said her words didn't make me harder than I already was.

As I read more of her words and saw my name on her screen, I slowly released my grip on her hands. Her hands shook as they went back to the keys on the keyboard.

"I'm just having a hard time with this scene." She swallowed hard again, her voice barely audible.

"Care to talk about it?" I asked, resting my hands on her shoulders and gently massaging them.

"I don't think you're going to want to help me write a sex scene, Brody." Her voice was so restricted, her body stiffening under my touch.

My hands went from her shoulders down her back, massaging gently. "You seem tense, Cass," I said as I continued to rub her back.

"I'm okay." She jumped off the stool and walked to the other side of the kitchen, grabbing a glass and filling it with cold water.

I needed to take her, the sexual tension in this room was killing me and her, I know it was. We'd been dancing around one another like a couple of high school kids for the past couple of weeks now. I walked over to where she was and slowly wrapped my arm around her waist, pulling her back, so she was resting against my chest.

"I don't know, it may be fun to try to help you write one. I mean, I've never done it before, but I have some ideas." I pulled her hair away from her neck and studied her creamy flesh.

She ran her hand over my forearm and down to my hand, resting hers on mine. I watched as her chest rose and fell in fast, short breaths.

"Funny, this is exactly the way my characters are standing in the scene I'm writing," she managed to choke out.

"I know, remember I just read some of it. Is this where you're stuck?" I whispered in her ear, my lips brushing against the outer edge of her earlobe.

"How did you know?" I couldn't miss the tremble in her soft voice.

"Cause that's where you stopped writing," I whispered.

I placed my other hand around her and placing tiny kisses on the side of her neck. I felt her shake as I continued. It was when I hit her ear and took her lobe between my lips, I heard her moan my name.

"What is it, Cass?"

"Brody, don't do this."

"Why not? It's called research," I said, my lips grazing her ear again.

"Because I'm not going to be able to say no to you," she said breathless, leaning her head back against my shoulder, exposing her neck to me.

I took my other hand and moved the material of her robe, so I could place it inside her bathrobe, running my hand across the flat of her soft stomach.

"Then don't say no." I felt her shudder under my touch. "All you need to do is use your imagination, Cass," I whispered.

As I pulled her in closer, I could feel my erection rub against her. Releasing her a bit, she turned in my arms. The soft pink blush on her cheeks had made its way down her chest, and the way her pupils dilated as her eyes locked with mine gave away everything she was feeling. She wanted this just as much as I did, there was no doubt. I didn't give her a moment to protest or tell me to stop, I crashed into her with such force, wrapping her in my arms. I swept my tongue against hers and ran my hands down her body, gripping her ass and pulling her as close to me as possible. I wanted her to feel me, to know how badly I wanted her. I'd had enough of hiding.

I pulled away from her lips and studied her eyes as I slowly traveled my hands back up and under her robe. At first, she didn't move, but then she wrapped her arms around my neck, her body trembling as her mouth met mine. She let another light moan escape as my fingers danced across her bare skin. When I picked her up, she wrapped her legs around my waist, and I carried her down the hall to her bedroom.

Dropping her onto the bed, I stopped and stood, looking at her lying before me, her dark hair framing her innocent looking face. I knelt onto the bed and pulled the ties on her bathrobe, letting it fall open. Exposing nothing more than her stomach, I bent down and kissed her bare belly. Her fingers ran through my hair. I stood, letting my sweats slide off my body. I caught her eyes drop from my face to my waist and widen as she saw the tip of my cock peeking out from the waistband of my boxers. Her eyes slowly traveled back up my body, finally meeting mine as I placed one knee between her legs.

I reached forward and pushed her robe open, both of my hands grazing her hardened nipples. Her back arched at my touch, and I leaned down and took a nipple into my mouth, rolling my tongue around it, sucking it into my mouth while I gently pinched the other one between my fingers. She let out a loud moan as I gently ran my teeth over her.

Kissing my way up to her neck, finally meeting her mouth, I was getting a little worried because she still hadn't touched me. I looked into her eyes, pleading with her.

"Put your hands on me." I could tell she was hesitant

maybe even a little afraid, but she finally placed her hands on my shoulders. As I swept my tongue against her, her hands fell away from me again. I pulled my lips away and looked her straight in the eyes, those beautiful blue eyes. "Don't be afraid to touch me, Cass, I want you," I whispered.

"I want you, Brody," she whispered, but her hands didn't move. I moved away from her, kicking off my boxers and watched as she sat up and removed her bathrobe, her eyes meeting my painful erection. With my hands on her hips, I slowly slid her panties down her body, my fingers skimming her legs, causing her skin to pebble.

I pushed her legs open, taking in her silky bare flesh. Kneeling back on the bed, I met her lips again, this time while I ran my fingers over her pussy. She moaned into my mouth as my fingers started circling her clit. I slid my fingers through her wetness and slid two fingers deep inside her, her moans getting louder as I sucked her bottom lip into my mouth.

At the sound of her moan, I knew I couldn't take it anymore, I needed her to touch me. I took her hand and placed it on my cock. At first, I thought I had burned her, she moved her hand away so fast. I took her hand again and placed it on me. She didn't move at first, but then I felt her thumb start rubbing the large bead of pre-cum around the head. She ran her hand down my shaft, squeezing before she loosened her grip. I was so worked up, I could feel myself about to lose control. I pulled my fingers from her heat and took hold of both her wrists, pinning them to the mattress above her head while I climbed between her legs, letting her calves rest on either side of my thighs.

"I hope you're ready for me baby," I moaned as I lined myself up at her entrance. She bit her lower lip as she watched me. Running the tip of my cock through her wetness, I could barely take the pressure of sliding into her tightness. I went as slow as I could, so she could feel every possible inch of me before I buried myself into her heat as deep as I could possibly go. She let out a cry of pain as I held myself inside of her, not moving.

"You okay? I didn't hurt you, did I?" I whispered in her ear, sucking her earlobe into my mouth.

"Go slow, Brody. You're bigger than I remember." Her voice was thick with emotion.

I wrapped her in my arms, holding her as I gently but deeply and forcefully pumped into her. It wasn't long before I felt her tightening around me, moaning my name in my ear. A couple deeper thrusts and a thunderous, uncontrollable, wave of pleasure ripped through me as I emptied myself into her.

As soon as the throbbing calmed, I slid out of her. I pulled back the duvet and sheet and picked her up, laying her down into the warm bed. I headed into the adjoining bathroom and got a wet cloth to clean her.

Once that was done I covered her body with the blankets.

"You stay here. I'll be right back."

She let out a beautiful, sleepy little moan as I left the room. I wasn't long, throwing a couple more logs into the fire and shutting the lights off. I walked back down to the bedroom and crawled in beside her, placing one arm under her pillow, the other wrapped around her waist, pulling her tightly against me. I wanted her to know tonight hadn't been a mistake, that it was okay to fall asleep in my arms, comfortable and safe.

Chapter Nineteen

Cass

I grabbed two mugs from the cupboard, waiting for the coffee to finish brewing. It was eight, I had already been up for a couple of hours, and Brody was still sleeping. I turned the radio on, soft Christmas music playing the background.

I hummed to myself as I removed the steaming pot of hot coffee and poured myself a mug. I was just about to take my mug back over to the computer when my phone pinged with a message.

I grabbed it off the counter, and my stomach flipped when I saw Ray's name flash across my screen. I had felt a wave of relief this morning I didn't need to see him for a couple of weeks, especially after what happened between Brody and me last night. There was no way I would be able to face Ray anytime soon. I didn't read or respond to the message. Instead, I turned my phone off, something that wasn't odd for me on a Sunday.

I picked my mug up and carried it over to the table where my laptop was and sat down. I opened the program I always use for writing and started to reread what I had written last night. As soon as I got to the part I had been working on, my thoughts went back to us in the kitchen. I squeezed my inner thighs together—I could still feel Brody firmly planted deep inside of me. I could still feel every touch, every kiss, and I still heard every tender whisper he had spoken. He was rough but gentle and tender, all at the same time. He had been perfect, and I had loved the way I felt his muscles tense when he came. The more I thought about it, the more I started to feel that familiar ache of want between my legs.

I tore my eyes away from the computer and looked to the bare tree standing in my living room. I could feel the tears creeping in. Everything had been so beautiful, and yet something, somewhere deep in my soul, told me I had to be careful, there was a good chance he would be gone before I knew it. The hard part for me was even though I didn't want to admit my feelings even to myself, I knew right where my heart lay. I needed to be careful with this whole situation, or I was going to get really hurt.

I got up from the table and walked over to the tree. Closing my eyes, I leaned in and took a big deep breath, smelling the fresh evergreen. I used to the love that smell. It had been so long since I had smelled it, I took another deep inhale. I felt like I could breathe that scent in forever.

I stood there, getting lost in my memories, listening to the soft music playing in the background. I was a million miles away when I felt two large, strong hands wrap around my waist, causing me to jump a little.

"Good morning," his deep, sexy, sleep filled voice greeted me as he pulled me back against his warm body and kissed my neck tenderly.

I let my head fall to the side as he continued placing soft kisses down the side of my neck to my shoulder. I could feel myself starting to get wet as the memory of last night ran through my mind.

"Brody, are you hungry? Did you want breakfast?"

A gentle hum came from his lips. "I'll eat you, that's all the breakfast I need." He ran his hands up under my shirt, cupping my breasts.

I turned and met his lips as he pulled me into him. I pulled away from him and went to step toward the kitchen when he grabbed me and picked me up throwing me over his shoulder.

I let out a loud laugh. "Brody, put me down."

"Nope, you're coming with me." He smacked me on the ass and carried me down the hall toward the bedroom.

Chapter Twenty

We drove down to town together in Brody's truck. The roads were rather slippery, and he didn't trust my car even though I had driven it a thousand times on roads like this.

"For dating a mechanic, you would think he would make sure you have good winter tires on your car, Cass. Until I can get snow tires ordered and put on your car, I'll drive you back and forth to work." Brody pulled in behind the back of the store and shut his truck off.

"Thanks, but really the tires are fine on my car, Brody."

"Cass, please, they are not fine. I want you to be safe, and these roads are bad."

Even though his comments stung, at least he cared which was more than I could say for Ray. I, of course, had Ray put the four almost five-year-old winter tires on my car. He told me they were still fine, I didn't drive far enough for it to matter, but I didn't let Brody know that.

"So, tell me more about this book drive."

"Well, the Coldhaven Fire Department had a really tragic fire last year, and five firefighters died. I know some of those families personally since moving here, and I really wanted to find a way to give back. At first, I was going to give a percentage of my sales over Christmas, but I'm still struggling, so I came up with the book drive idea. What books don't sell, I'll donate to the local library, and the money from the ones that do sell will go to the families."

"Wow, I had no idea. Well, I'm not sure if you know or not, but I did sign up to help with the book drive. The coffee shop across the street had a sign-up sheet, and I filled it out before I knew it was you."

"I know, Maggie told me," I smiled.

"Good, so use me any way you like. I'm all yours," he said, lifting his eyebrows and smiling.

As soon as those three little words fell from his lips, I suddenly wished he was really all mine. I met his eyes, a slight blush creeping over me.

"What is it, Cass?"

I shook my head. "Let's go before it starts to snow," I said, jumping from the front seat of the truck out into the cold. There was no way I could answer him, not yet. I didn't want to scare him away again.

As we approached the back door, I found about twelve boxes of books piled up outside the door. The church had already been there to donate the books they had collected. Brody carried those boxes inside while I cleared a couple more shelves and a table to be able to display more books.

He dropped a couple of boxes on the table and continued bringing in the others, putting them in the small storage room. I wouldn't be able to take any more donations until I had gone through some of these boxes. I didn't want to have a ton left over, and I didn't carry a used section in the store.

"I figure the day of the actual book fair, I can always discount at the end of the day. Like the last hour or something, I can do a bag for five or something."

"That sounds good, Cass. Do you have many other volunteers?"

"You."

"That's it?"

"Yes, Maggie is sending her daughters over to help with collecting money, but you are it, otherwise."

"Well, you can count on me, I'll be here."

We continued working for a couple of hours before he finally dragged me away.

"It's your day off Cass. Let's go grab the things we need for the tree and head home."

I took a step back and looked at what I had accomplished. "Does it look okay?"

"It looks great." He walked up behind me and took my hands in his. "You can fuss over this tomorrow, it's time to go." He kissed the back of my neck and pulled me away from the table toward the back door of the shop.

Chapter Twenty-One

"I think it's in that one there, Brody." I pointed to the blue tote up on the top shelf in the garage.

Brody grabbed the step ladder and climbed up, pulling the tote down I had pointed at. He sat it down on the floor and tucked the ladder away, and I went to pick up the tote.

"Leave it, I got it, it's heavy." He bent down, picking up the tote and brought it inside, dropping it on the floor in front of the tree.

"Alright, before we get started, let's get in some comfy clothes, you get the wine, and let's decorate this baby," Brody said, grinning at me.

He took off to his room, and I headed into the kitchen. Neither of us had spoken a word to one another about last night or this morning, and except that single kiss this afternoon, Brody had basically kept his hands off me. I wasn't sure how I felt about it, and I did my best not to read into it.

I grabbed a chilled bottle of white from the fridge and two glasses, dropping them off on the table in the living room before heading to my room. Changing quickly into a pair of shorts and a tank top, I made my way back out to the living room to find Brody starting to put the new lights on the tree.

I stood and watched him from the doorway of the hall, reminded of Jackson—he had always put the lights on the tree. I blinked away the tears that had started to burn my eyes and poured us some wine.

"Did we get a tree topper?"

"I think I have one, Brody, hang on." I searched through the tote from the garage, finally finding the angel Jackson had bought for me the first year we lived in the house buried in the bottom. Handing it to him, he placed it on top of the tree and continued with the lights. I stood staring up at the angel, remembering the night Jackson had surprised me with it. It brought tears to my eyes thinking of the smile on his face when I had seen it. I shook away the memory and started helping Brody with the lights. This was why I avoided Christmas, most of the memories were too painful to keep reliving every year, and if I could just pretend in my personal life it didn't exist, I didn't have to live with the pain.

The night went on like that, some decorations, especially the special ones almost bringing me to my knees. I didn't say anything, I didn't have to, I knew Brody could tell, but he tried tirelessly to keep me laughing. When the tree was completely decorated, we stood in front of it the lights flashing red, green, and yellow. I could feel him watching me, taking in my reaction. It had been three years since I had a tree in my living room. Aside from all the memories tonight brought up, I think I missed all the beautiful decorations.

Brody grabbed the remote, turning the TV to a radio channel. Silent Night had just started playing. He dropped the remote down beside where Missy was sleeping and slowly approached me. He grabbed my hands, placing one on his shoulder and pulled me into his arms.

"Care to dance with me?"

"I don't dance anymore, Brody." I started to pull away out of his embrace.

"Sure, you do." He grabbed me, slowly pulling me into his arms. We started slowly swaying in time to the music in front of the tree. I loved how our bodies fit together, and how the feeling of being held in his arms again was like a dream come true. I rested my head on his shoulder and closed my eyes, breathing in his masculine scent. "See you still dance."

When the song was over, we stopped moving, a long kiss on my forehead bringing me back to the moment. I lifted my head and looked into his eyes, hungry with need. He lifted my chin with his hand and crashed down onto my lips.

His hands gripping me under the ass, he picked me up, wrapping my legs around his waist, carrying me over to the couch, and sat down with me straddling his lap. He continued kissing me as he leaned over to shut the light off. The soft music filled the room as I concentrated on him, the light from the fire dancing off his skin.

When we parted, he stared into my eyes and placed both his hands on my cheeks, pulling me gently toward him. He kissed me, and I could feel something very different in this kiss than I could last night or even this morning. It was deeper, slower, and filled with a feeling I couldn't describe. When he pulled away, his strong hand still cupped my cheek. As he looked into my eyes, his hid nothing.

"I wasn't going to say anything, but I haven't been able to get last night or this morning out of my head."

I felt myself start to blush, then his lips crashed into mine again.

"Is it completely wrong that I want to take you again?"

I hesitated, not sure how to answer him. It was so wrong, but as I looked into his eyes, I shook my head no and bit my bottom lip. As much as he wanted to take me, I wanted him to. I felt his fingers dance along my inner thigh, getting closer to my center. I closed my eyes, waiting for him to touch me, but he pulled his hand back.

"Don't tease me," I moaned.

His hand moved back up my thigh, this time getting closer to my center than before, then pulled away again. "Why not?"

I looked into his eyes, his pupils dilated as he looked up at me with a soft smile.

"Because it's not fair!" I lifted my body off the couch to bite his bottom lip as my hand reached down and ran my hand over his hard cock one time only, then pulled away, listening to the groan that left his throat.

Again, I felt his hand dancing along the skin of my inner thigh, this time though, he reached into the leg of my shorts and ran his fingers through my center, teasing my clit. A moan escaped me as his lips crashed down on mine. He stopped, and when I was about to voice my complaint, he buried two fingers deep inside of me.

"Is that better, baby?"

When I felt myself starting to tighten around his fingers, he removed his fingers and picked me up off the couch, carrying me down the hall. He placed me down on the floor by the bed and pulled my shirt over my head.

Then he slowly pulled my shorts down, kissing down my body, until they fell in a puddle at my feet. I ran my hands down his strong chest to the waistband of his sweats and pulled them down, his cock springing free. He pulled me down onto the bed, kissing me slow and deep. Lying on his back he gripped my waist, holding on to me while I straddled him. Placing himself at my opening, he guided himself inside of me, bringing me down on top of him as he relaxed against the mattress. I felt so full this way, and he waited to let me adjust to him.

With our eyes locked, I slowly started to rock my hips. He took his hands and ran them down my breasts to my belly, finally resting them once again on my hips. I loved feeling him deep inside of me.

He sat up on the edge of the bed, picked me up and lay me on my back, thrusting into me deeply. I wrapped my legs around his waist and moaned deeply as he continued to pound into me. We came hard and fast, Brody collapsing on me.

Chapter Twenty-Two

Cass

I had just finished cleaning up the small kitchen in the back of the store, so I sat down at the table, opened my laptop, and started writing. While we were waiting for the new tires he had ordered me to come in, Brody had religiously driven me every day to the shop and picked me up. Today, I had to wait for Brody. He had been called out on a call late this morning and was on his way back. He had messaged me just as I was closing to let me know he would be here a little after six.

My phone pinged with a message while I was checking Amazon for a couple of Christmas gifts for Brody.

BRODY: I should be there soon, just unloading the truck, hang tight

ME: No worries, I'm not going anywhere

I smiled to myself and put the phone down on the table and went back to writing. The familiar ping rang through the room once again.

BRODY: I can't wait to see you, been a long day, I need me some Cass time

ME: Makes two of us

BRODY: You need Cass time too? I really didn't want to have to share you

I smiled to myself and was just about to type out my response when my phone started to ring, and Ray's name flashed across my screen. I was almost paralyzed with fear. I had done a good job of answering his text messages, but I couldn't answer his call, he would hear my betrayal in my voice. I tried to ignore it, but he called again. He would know I was finished work and would more than likely be either just leaving the store or on my way home. When the phone rang for the third time in a row, I decided I didn't have a choice, I had to answer the phone and face him.

"Hello," I said quietly into the phone, trying to hide the shake in my voice.

"There you are. I've called three times, where were you?"

I looked around the tiny room and shut down the lid of my laptop. There was no use in trying to write anymore waiting for Brody because I knew after this call, the words wouldn't flow.

"Sorry, I was just in the shower, I left my phone in the living room."

"You're home already?"

I glanced at the time, I was cutting it close to have been home and in the shower by six.

"It was quiet today, I wasn't feeling all that well, so I closed a little early." I doubted he would buy that either.

"You closed early?" he asked in disbelief. "Cass, I told you, you are burning the candle at both ends, I wish you would just drop this silly book stuff, get some rest."

I didn't want to hear it, so I changed the subject. "How's the trip going?"

"Good, I might be back earlier than I expected. The weather has been good." I felt my chest get tighter at the mere thought of him returning.

"Glad to hear," I choked.

"Are you guys done playing house yet?" I knew right away from his comment, he had been out drinking with some of his buddies.

"Ray, I told you, he's a friend. I won't have him stay in some back room at the fire station.

"So, knowing it bothers me, you'll have him stay with you instead. Nice."

I said nothing and got quiet. I certainly wasn't innocent, and at this point, I wasn't proud of what I had done, but I knew how I felt. I twirled the cord to my laptop in between my fingers.

"Ray, I'm sorry, but I just can't let him do that, I explained things to you."

"What you explained to me is that you have feelings for the guy, a guy might I add you have a prior history with. Don't you think that makes me worry? Why are you so quiet?"

"I'm not feeling all that well."

"I'm not going to have to rearrange any teeth, am I?"

"Ray, stop it."

The line went quiet for a couple of minutes. "Should I be worried, Cass? Am I going to lose you to him?"

I swallowed hard, tears coming to my eyes. Rearrange teeth, no you won't have to do that, but I fear you may kill him or possibly me when you find out what's gone on between us.

"Everything's fine. No need to worry."

I heard the back door to the shop open and felt a blast of cold air.

"Cass?" Brody called from the door.

I popped my head around the corner. As soon as I saw him, I gave him a gentle smile and held my finger over my lips.

"Is he there Cass?" Rays voice came over the phone blaring in my ear.

"No."

"I heard him, Cass, why are you lying?" he demanded.

"I'm not, it was the TV, Ray."

"Whatever."

"I'm not doing this with you right now, Ray. I've got to go." Brody looked at me, his expression changing from happy to pissed off. He waved his fingers in a 'give me' motion, pointing at the phone, but I shook my head and locked eyes with him.

"You're not wanting to do what right now, Cass? If I find out anything has gone on between you while I've been gone, I swear to god that man won't be walking another day in his life."

I didn't have anything to say. The tears welled in my eyes, finally spilling over and tumbling down my cheeks. Brody walked over and pulled me against him, gently brushing away my tears.

"Cass, I'm fucking talking to you."

Brody looked into my eyes and slowly took the cell phone from my hand and ended the call. Throwing it on the table, he wrapped his arms around me in a tight embrace. I rested my head on his chest and let out a deep sob.

"He's going to be so mad at me for that."

"Nope, he deserved that. I could hear him yelling before I was even near you. Now, let's go home."

I glanced down at the table, my cell phone vibrating away, Ray's name flashing on the screen. "I need to get that."

I stood frozen, not moving from Brody's embrace, just staring down at the phone. He picked up my phone, turning the power off, silencing the noise, and placed it in his pocket. Then he lay two fingers on the side of my jaw and placed the gentlest kiss on my lips, sweeping his tongue through my mouth. Soon, I forgot all about what had just happened and let myself get lost in his kiss.

Chapter Twenty-Three

Cass

We were supposed to be cleaning up after dinner, but instead, I found myself with my arms pinned above my head and my back pressed against the wall as Brody continued his assault on my lips. He swept his tongue through my mouth and ground his erection against my leg.

"Fuck, I feel like a teenager again," he moaned into my mouth.

I fought to get a hand loose, and when I did, I opened the button on his jeans. There was just enough room, I could reach my hand inside his pants and stroke him through his boxers.

"God Cass, that feels amazing." He kissed the side of my neck and gripped my ass, pulling me closer against him.

I opened my eyes and caught my cell phone, sitting on the counter, vibrating away. I eyed my cell phone, Ray's name flashing across the screen, distracting me.

"Leave it alone, Cass," Brody murmured into my neck. "Get lost in me."

"Brody, please. I should answer it."

"You should shut the thing off, he doesn't deserve you." He groaned as he ran his hands over my body.

"Brody, we should really clean up this kitchen."

"I'd rather be right where I am," he whispered as he leaned down and bit my nipple through my thin t-shirt.

I threw my head back against the wall, letting myself do exactly as he asked—get lost in him.

"Come join me in the shower," he said, meeting my lips again.

"No go, I'm going to clean up here, then we'll relax."

He pouted like a schoolboy, kissed me one final time, then made his way down the hall to shower and get changed. It took me a few minutes to calm my beating heart, but the throbbing ache between my legs wasn't going to subside until I was screaming his name. I shut the thought out of my head and started cleaning up the mess we had made from dinner. I placed the final pan into the dishwasher and started wiping down the counters when my phone vibrated again. I glanced down the hall and could still hear the shower running. I eyed the phone again, finally grabbing it off the counter and answered it.

"Hello."

"It's about fucking time you picked up the damn phone."

"Don't be angry, Ray."

"I'm not angry, I'm furious. Why are you ignoring my calls? Were you busy... with him?"

What was I going to say, *Sorry, Ray, I couldn't answer the phone because Brody had his tongue in my mouth*? "I left my phone in my purse, and I didn't hear it ring," I lied.

"Listen, I've been giving it some thought, Cass, I think I'm going to stay down here a little longer, sort out how I feel about you. Give you a little space and time."

My eyes burned as I listened to his words.

"I think it's the right thing to do," his voice cracked as it came over the phone.

I sat down on the couch in the living room. I didn't have anything to say, I knew he was right, it was the right thing to do.

"I'll come see you when I return."

I still couldn't speak, the words wanted to come, but my throat wouldn't open to allow them to come out.

"Goodbye, Cass." The line went dead. I covered my mouth with my hand. I was so torn, I didn't know what to do. I wiped the tears from my eyes and heard the water shut off in the bathroom. I needed to get some control over myself before Brody came back out here.

I powered down my phone and put it on the charger. I went into the storage room across from my bedroom. I was still looking for a small box of decorations I had packed away I couldn't find, and this was the only place I had left to look. I walked into the room and looked at the mountain of boxes that still needed to be unpacked. How I had managed to live here for three years and not unpack a single, solitary box in this room was beyond me. I grabbed a couple boxes off the pile and started to root through them.

"What are you doing?" I heard his deep sexy voice from the doorway.

"Looking for those decorations for the tree," I sighed.

Brody took a step in the room and helped me lift a rather heavy box down to the floor. I opened it and frowned. Inside, right on top, sat a wooden, locked box with my name engraved on the top. I had never seen it before. I removed the box and set it beside me.

"What's that?" he asked.

"I don't know, I've never seen this before. Jackson used to have a box sort of like this, nothing engraved on the top of his, but I haven't seen it in years. If I recall correctly, he either lost or broke it shortly after we got married. I'll have to ask my mom where she found this, she must have packed it. She was the one who did most of the packing when I moved." I continued sorting through the box, coming across more of Jackson's belongings.

"Maybe it's in this one, Cass."

"Which?"

"The one labeled Christmas." I looked over my shoulder and saw his smile.

"Perhaps," I laughed. I closed the box I had been sorting through, leaving the mysterious locked box on the floor to take to my room and turned to go through the box Brody had opened. Sure enough, there sat the small box of decorations I had been looking for.

"Could you take these to the living room, please? I'll be there in a minute," I said, running my hand over his back.

He leaned in and tenderly kissed me. "Sure thing, I'll pour us some wine."

I nodded, and Brody took the box of decorations from my hand and left the room. I closed the box, bent to pick up the little wooden box from the floor, and took it into my bedroom, setting it on my dresser. I tugged on the lock to see if it would open, but it was secured. I had no idea where I would find the key.

I glanced back at the little box again before I shut off the bedroom light. I had a small box of loose keys somewhere in the kitchen I would have to sort through, but for now, it would have to wait.

Chapter Twenty-Four

Cass

There was something about the way Brody held me that had always made me feel so safe and secure. I didn't know if it was just because we fit so perfectly against one another or because when he held me, I knew it was with every fiber of his being.

When I opened my eyes, the room was completely dark, the blackout curtains drawn tight. I checked the clock, it was already five. I didn't want to get out of bed, but I had to get to the store, and the way the wind was howling outside, told me it was probably storming, and it would take me longer than usual to get there.

Brody kissed me on the shoulder, pulling me tighter

into him. I could only stay in his arms for another ten minutes at most, or else I would probably be late. My eyes drifted shut as I felt his hands slide down my bare body. He had kept me up most of the night, not that I regretted that, but I was tired. His hand stopped on my hip, and he pulled me back against his hardness.

"Don't start, I'm sore, and I have to get up to get ready for work."

He started kissing my neck, his hand inching toward the inside of my thighs.

"Open your legs," he breathed into my ear.

A chill ran through my body as I leaned against his chest. He propped himself up on his elbow and met my lips, his fingers running over my aching clit. I was super sensitive and gripped his hand to stop him as he started rubbing in small circles.

"What is it?"

"I'm a little sore and a lot sensitive."

"That's okay, I have a treat for you," he chuckled as he kissed me deeper, moving down to my neck stopping at my chest to suck my hardened nipples. He continued kissing down my stomach, stopping when he moved to the insides of my thighs. My back arched off the mattress as I felt his tongue run down my slit and back up, sucking my clit into his mouth. He kept his hands firmly planted on the inside of my thighs, holding them open while I grabbed hold of my pillow and arched my back off the mattress.

"Be a good girl, Cass, I want you to come on my tongue. I want to taste you." He moaned, blowing gentle breaths across my wetness, then pressing his tongue against my clit.

"Fuck, Brody, you've got to stop." My hands ran over his head, my fingers pulling and gripping his hair.

"No fucking way." He sucked my clit into his mouth, gently taking it between his teeth and running his tongue over it.

I couldn't hold it back anymore, yet another orgasm smashed into me. I screamed out his name as he continued lapping at my center.

I lay there, breathing hard, my eyes closed, trying to come down from my orgasm. When I opened my eyes, Brody was studying me a soft smile on his lips.

"You good?"

"Hmmm, yes," I giggled. Looking at the clock, it was now almost six, and I jumped out of bed. "I'm going to be so late, Brody." I spun around the room, grabbing clothes from my dresser and closet as he lay in bed chuckling, his arms behind his head, looking awfully proud of himself.

"Yeah, but you can't tell me it wasn't worth it, and you're the boss, you can be late," he winked. I stopped what I was doing, walked over, and kissed him hard.

"What about you?" I ran my hand down his stomach, playing with the hair just below his navel.

"You can owe me tonight," he smiled at me as he threw the covers off himself, grabbing his sweatpants off the floor. I couldn't help but take him in. "Get yourself ready, I'll go make us some breakfast."

Five minutes after he was gone, he came back into the bedroom calling my name.

"Yeah," I shouted from the bathroom where I had just gotten out of a hot shower.

"You aren't going anywhere, Cass, massive storm outside. Highway patrol has shut all the roads up here." He walked into the bathroom, ripped the towel from my hand and picked me up, throwing me over his shoulder.

"It's time for you to reward me." I laughed as he grabbed hold of me, opened the shower door, and pulled me inside.

Chapter Twenty-Five

We laid in bed together, wrapped up in each other. We had spent the entire late part of the morning in bed after our shower. My head was on his chest, fighting sleep as I listened to his heart beating in my ear, his fingers tracing tiny circles on my shoulder. In the distance, I heard the phone ring, finally stopping, only to start up again.

"I should get that, it could be one of my customers," I said, sitting up.

"No way, you're not going anywhere, they can leave a message," he said pulling me back down and into him. "I want you all day, right in my arms." He pressed a soft kiss to my lips, his tongue swiping through my mouth, my body going limp as I kissed him back.

I ran my hand down his chest, over his abs, until I reached his cock. Taking it in my hand, I let it slip through my fingers. It wasn't long before he was hard.

"I'll be right back," I smiled and crawled under the covers. I heard him inhale as I ran my tongue up his shaft, taking him into my mouth, running my tongue around the head of his cock.

"Fuck," he moaned. I heard the familiar ringing of his cell phone, then he put his hand on my head, trying to get my attention, but I didn't stop what I was doing. "Cass... stop," he said, breathless.

I continued sucking while rubbing his shaft, ignoring his plea.

"Cass, stop, the fire department is calling."

I pulled my mouth away from his cock, crawled up, and poked my head out from under the covers, grinning at him. Once he answered the phone, I ran my tongue around the head of his cock a couple of times before taking him fully into my mouth again.

"You need me to come now? But the highway patrol has shut all the roads up here," he said, trying not to breathe too hard. He laid back against the pillow, eyes closed, half listening to the other end while I sucked on his cock.

"Alright, give me some time, I'll be there."

He hung up the phone and placed his hand on the back of my head, pulling my hair back away from my face so he could watch me take him in my mouth.

"You are a bad girl." He moaned to the ceiling. I could feel his cock throbbing, so I took him deeper in my mouth. I could feel his muscles tensing as I took him to the back of my throat just in time for him to come. His body finally relaxed into the mattress, and he laid there, breathing hard, stroking my back gently.

"You have to go, don't you?" I whispered, resting my head on his stomach when his breathing finally calmed.

"Yep. Two skiers have gone missing sometime last night up at the resort, they need all the help they can get to find them. With this storm, they could freeze to death if out in the elements much longer," he explained, pushing my hair out of my face, looking into my eyes.

"I don't want you to go," I pouted.

"There is no place I'd rather be than right here with you, but duty calls. These people need help, Cass."

I nodded, a funny feeling coming over me, a wave of nausea passing through me at the thought of him leaving.

"How long will you be gone?"

"Until we find them. They're calling in help from all over, so hopefully, not long, but you never know. I don't want you to worry though, I'll be with other guys, we don't search alone. You know that."

I lifted myself off him and let him get out of bed,

watching his naked ass as he walked toward the shower. He was ready in minutes, and I walked him to the door in my bathrobe, fighting anxiety and tears every step of the way. The cold air hit me as he opened the door.

"Oh, and Cass, no peeking under that tree," he said, nodding toward the two wrapped boxes under the tree. He leaned in, kissing me hard. I watched as he pulled his hood up over his head and headed toward his truck.

The memory that ran through my mind as I watched him disappear out of the driveway was enough to make me want to vomit. I felt like I was close to reliving the worst day of my life all over again, this time with a completely different man.

A couple hours later, I was showered and dressed, sitting at the table, working on my book, a steaming hot cup of tea beside me and Missy in my lap. Brody had been gone for three hours by now and had sent me a text, letting me know he had just arrived at the ski lodge.

Brody: Keep the house warm in case the power goes out. Get some wood in. Whatever you do, do not go out in this.

I glanced over at the wood and saw I only had about a dozen or so pieces left inside.

Me: Doing that know, be safe.

Brody: This may not be the best way or time to tell you but you need to know, I love you

I stared down at the screen and read over those three little words. Blinking again to make sure they were there that funny feeling returning to my stomach again. My hands shook as I deleted the first three words I had typed, correcting it, I pressed send.

Me: Can't wait for you to come home.

I sat the phone down on the table and suddenly, what I had typed struck me. Home, the word hit me, it was his home, and I sincerely couldn't wait until he was back here. I waited for a reply, but nothing came. I waited a little more, then I got up, grabbed my coat and boots and headed out to get some wood, just like he had asked. I opened the back door and stepped out into a blizzard. I couldn't see more than a couple feet in front of me for the blowing snow. I made my way over to the woodpile, loaded up the wood sling, taking it in the house. I made close to a dozen trips, then shut and locked the back door, pulling the curtains across the sliding doors. I was just piling more wood in the fire when I realized Brody was out in this nightmare of a storm. That was when the realization really set in.

I sipped my tea, trying to calm the panic rising in me,

but he wouldn't leave my mind. It was bad out, and a storm like this could trap someone for hours, even days up here. I knew he was fully trained, but I was still afraid I might never see him again. I grabbed my cell to see if he had responded, but there was nothing, so I sent another text off to him. "Answer me please," I whispered. After five minutes, I sent another. Again, nothing. I wanted to hear his voice, I knew that would calm the panic, and I was just about to call him, when I heard a loud knock on the front door.

I ran to the door with my heart in my throat, but as soon as I saw who was standing there, I felt the bile rise into my throat, and my heart sank into my gut.

"Well, are you going to invite me in or just leave me standing out here in the blowing snow?"

Chapter Twenty-Six

Cass

I looked at Ray, the cold air blowing into the house and couldn't move.

"Cass, you look like you've seen a ghost. Are you going to let me in?"

"Of course." I swallowed hard and stood off to the side, making room for him, shutting the door behind him.

"It's fucking freezing out, this storm came out of nowhere. I was on my way home but thought I better stop in and make sure you were okay."

"I'm good, Ray. Really. I have wood, a fire, and food in the fridge." I didn't want him to stay, my mind a million miles away, worried about Brody.

"Well, I'm here, so I may as well start by apologizing for my behavior the other night." He shrugged out of his coat and took off his boots. "Mind if I come in to get warm?" he asked, his eyes meeting mine.

It looked as if it didn't matter whether I wanted him there or not, he had already made up his mind, he was staying. He headed over to the wood stove and warmed his cold hands in front of the fire.

"Where's your buddy?" he asked looking around the room.

I hung his coat up on a hook, then walked over to the table and closed my laptop. We had enough to talk about, I didn't need to listen to his disapproval about my writing.

"He was called to search for two people who are missing up at the ski resort."

"Aww, so we're alone then." He walked over and placed his now warm hands on my waist, pulling me in for a kiss. I went through the motions, but other than that felt nothing.

When his lips parted from mine, I pulled away, turning out of his arms. "Do you want a tea or coffee?" I questioned, moving toward the kitchen.

"Coffee would be good, thanks," he answered. I could sense the disappointment in his voice, but he didn't let on that anything was wrong.

"How's the book drive been going?"

"Okay, I guess, this storm isn't going to help matters.

It may shut us down for a day or two. Highway patrol shut everything down this morning. It couldn't have come at a worse time."

"How much have you raised so far?"

"I'm just shy of five thousand," I said, pouring him a cup of steaming coffee.

"Well, that's good then, they should be happy with what they get. I mean, after all, it's more than they had to start."

I knew how Ray felt about me doing this. Sure, he liked the fact I wanted to help, but in his mind, if all I collected was five dollars, it would be good enough. I felt as though it didn't matter to him that I knew all too well the truth of what these families had been going through. Single mothers trying to raise children on a very limited budget, most of them wouldn't be getting a Christmas this year. At least with the money, they would be able to have a decent holiday meal and a gift for each child under the tree with a little money left over. It mattered to me what I raised. I knew these families well and knew they were struggling to make ends meet, just like I had, and I hadn't had extra mouths to feed.

"Yes, Ray, I suppose your right. However, the more I can give to them, the happier I will be. It matters to me." I set my mug down and grabbed a pot to thaw my soup.

"Is that what you're having for dinner? Maybe I'll join you. After all, it's getting later than I thought." He glanced at his watch and plunked down on the stool, sipping his coffee, watching my every move.

"Sure." I dumped the contents of the half-frozen soup into the pot and turned on the stove. I was on edge and could barely even look at him after all that had happened while he'd been gone.

We ate in complete silence. Every move I made, I could feel his eyes drilling deeper into me. I cleared the bowls from the counter and placed them in the dishwasher, then busied myself making another pot of coffee. I couldn't get my mind off Brody out in the cold, and I half listened as Ray went on and on about his trip. I glanced at the time, it was already eight. I knew once Ray left, I wouldn't be getting much sleep. I would need to spend the night writing to keep myself distracted from the bad thoughts I was having. I filled the coffee maker with water, then filled up the filter with fresh coffee grounds.

Ray was making me super uncomfortable. I tried to put the fact he was watching me out of my mind. I glanced over my shoulder at him before going to the deep freeze to put the coffee grounds back in the freezer. As I shut the freezer door I felt his hands slip around my waist and his lips at the back of my neck.

"I missed you," he whispered. "I couldn't wait to get back here to you. I'm glad we have the house to ourselves." He ran his hands up my body, taking my breasts into his hands while kissing the side of my neck. I closed my eyes, holding back tears, my mind going to Brody and the events of this morning. At that moment, I wished he was here instead of out there, and he was the one who was behind me, holding me, kissing me, and touching me.

I stood frozen, feeling nothing but violated as he continued his assault on me. He ran his hands back down my stomach and slid them into my pants, running his fingers over my panties.

"You're wet already, baby," he whispered, taking my ear into his mouth.

"Ray, stop," I cried out, but he ignored me.

I could feel his arousal pressing into me. He plunged his fingers inside my panties, dipping them into my wetness.

"Fuck, you're making my mouth water, baby, I can't wait to taste you." He picked me up, throwing me over his shoulder.

"Ray, please, I can't."

He smacked me on the ass. "What do you mean you can't?"

"I got my period today." I lied.

Ray leaned in and kissed me. "That doesn't bother me, baby, you know that."

"It does me, so can we wait, please?"

His forehead met mine, the look in his eyes told me he was questioning my refusal. "If we must. I probably should get home and unload the truck. You sure you got everything you need here?" He glanced over his shoulder at the pile of wood I had brought in.

"I believe so," I nodded.

"It's fine, don't worry, once I get the truck unloaded I'll come back over, and spend the night. I want to make sure you're fine."

"Of course."

Ray grabbed his jacket and threw on his boots. As soon as he was gone, I ran to my cell and checked for any messages, but there was still nothing. I quickly typed out a *Wish you were here* and sat down for my last few minutes of solitude and started writing.

Before Ray returned, I quickly changed the sheets on my bed—they smelled of sex and Brody. Ray was coming back, no doubt spending the night, and there was no way to talk him out of it.

I lay awake, listening to the howling wind while Ray snored beside me. I kept my cell phone beside me on the night stand, watching for the screen to light up, signifying I had a message. I was trying not to worry, but after another two hours, there was still nothing.

I couldn't lay there anymore, so I got up, careful not to move the bed and took my phone out into the living room. The fire had died down, so I threw a couple more logs into the stove and went to make a cup of tea.

I quickly typed out a message to Brody.

Me: You there?

It was useless, I didn't know why I was torturing myself like this. He was out searching for these kids, he was safe and fine, I told myself. I poured the boiling water into my cup and that was when my screen lit up. I rubbed my eyes, at first thinking I was dreaming, but the message sat there, loud and clear.

Brody: Hey, baby, I'm here

Me: Are you coming home soon?

Brody: Still searching, just came back in to get warm and some food. I'm exhausted

Me: I'm glad you're okay. please come back to me

Brody: No worries, baby, I'm gonna get some sleep, have to be back out in a couple hours

Me: Dream of me

Brody: Always

I sat, staring at the words on my screen. What a mess I was in. The man I was in a relationship with was sound asleep down the hall, in the exact same bed not twenty-four hours ago, I had the best sex I think I'd ever had with Brody. Here I sat, texting the man I was in love with. My gut churned, everything had been fine until I opened the front door tonight and came face to face with reality.

My stomach turned at the thought of having to choose. I was going to crush one of them, and I would have to live with that. On one hand, Brody had walked away from me, leaving me to fend when I had needed him the most. How could I ever be certain that he wouldn't do it again?

Ray, on the other hand, had always helped, no matter what I had asked of him. However, he didn't treat me the way I should be treated, and he didn't support me in the things I did, things that were important to me.

I took my tea and laptop and curled up into my armchair with a blanket.

"Please tell me what to do, Jackson" I whispered into the air. "Give me a sign, any sign. It is Christmas after all." I started feverishly typing away, praying that somehow, he would answer me.

Chapter Twenty-Seven

Cass

The storm lasted two days straight. Brody still hadn't returned, the news said they were still searching for those two skiers. My stomach was in knots as I got ready for work. I had barely slept or eaten since Brody had left. I made sure Missy had enough food and water for today as I would be later tonight than normal.

I had just gotten to the shop and put the coffee on when Ray came in the back door.

"Morning Cass."

"Morning." I stepped out of the small kitchen, glancing at my watch. It was almost six. I had so much to do and a lot was weighing on my mind.

"I wanted to stop and drop off breakfast to you," he said, handing me a bag from the coffee shop.

"Thanks," I said, taking the bag but avoiding his eyes.

"Cass, is something wrong?"

"Why would you ask that?"

"You just don't seem yourself."

"I don't seem myself? You've got to be kidding. How can you even say that? I'm worried about Brody."

"Where is your lover? Thought he was supposed to be helping you?" he questioned.

I felt the tears burn my eyes. Once again, I didn't understand why he was doing this, anyone who had watched the news knew where they were.

"He's still searching," I answered, pouring a cup of coffee and heading into the front of the store.

I heard Rays footsteps follow behind me. I only had a couple hours to get everything ready to open. Not that there was that much to do, but the way I was feeling, it was going to take me a while.

"Didn't you hear? They were found yesterday in the early morning. However, three members of the search team are now missing."

My stomach dropped, and I suddenly felt sick.

"Did...Did they say who?" I could feel the tears welling in my eyes yet again.

"No names were given yet, they say they may be dead. They apparently went missing the first night."

I bolted to the bathroom, almost missing the toilet as I threw up the empty contents of my stomach. I ran cold water onto a cloth and put it up to the back of my neck to stop the room from spinning, but it did little good. Ray appeared in the mirror.

"What's the problem Cass."

He fucking knew what the problem was. Granted, he didn't know everything about my past, but he knew enough.

I knew enough that for searches like this, they took breaks often, switching up every couple of hours or so to get warm and eat. However, something wasn't right, and Ray passing it off the way he was, wasn't making it better.

"I haven't heard from Brody since that first night."

"Yeah, but that doesn't mean it's him. Maybe he just left you, Cass, you know like last time." It was then the tears started. I knew in my heart he wouldn't leave again, not after we made love, but Ray's words were making me second guess myself.

As the tears ran down my face, I could see Ray getting angrier by the second at my actions. Finally, without another word he marched out the back of the store, leaving me in silence.

The day went by slowly. It was almost closing time when May came through the front door.

"My dear, it's getting colder outside, did you hear it's

possible another storm is coming? I hope you're heading straight home after work."

"Hey, May. I am. How was the store today?" I asked, trying to take my mind off Brody.

"It was okay. Everyone was glad to be out and around. How are things going for the fundraiser?"

"Pretty good, May, so far I have raised a little under five thousand, just about a thousand per family."

"That is wonderful. I'm just going to take a peak and see what is there."

May walked over to the books on display, and I went back to searching my phone for any news, debating whether to call the fire department and find out what was really going on.

"Cassie, my dear, you look like you have the weight of the world on your shoulders. What is it?"

I swallowed hard, trying to hold back the tears that were threatening to fall. I had been good all day, but May was always so easy to talk to. My head fell into my hands.

"It's awful."

"What is it, dear?" I suddenly felt her arm around me, smoothing my hair, trying to comfort me.

"It's my friend, Brody, he went up to help search for those people, and now there are members of the rescue crew missing. I haven't heard from him in days."

"Oh, love. No tears, I am sure he's okay, probably just busy and exhausted."

"Well then, why does my gut tell me different, that he's in trouble, May?"

"What do you mean?"

"I can't lose him. If I lose him after I lost Jackson, it will be the end of me, May. I'm in love with him."

I had never heard the back door open, never heard the footsteps approaching the front of the store before the words fell out of my mouth, and I confided in May. When I looked up, Ray was standing behind us. The look on his face, the hurt in his eyes was enough to knock me in the gut.

"Ray! What are you doing here?"

"Apparently, I'm just in time to hear the truth, Cass."

May turned around and looked at Ray who stood looming over us. "Oh, Ray, I'm sure it's not what you think."

"I'm afraid it is, May. I'll see you later, Cass." Ray turned to walk back through the store and stopped just before stepping outside. "Oh, Cass, by the way I stopped by to let you know the names of the rescue workers were announced on the radio, Brody is one of them. They'll give up searching on Christmas Eve if they don't find them before that." He opened the door, stepped outside, and slammed it shut at the same time my heart shattered into a million and one pieces.

Chapter Twenty-Eight

Cass

May stayed with me after Ray left. She shut and locked the store while I sat with my face in my hands, my shoulders shaking. My stomach hurt, and my chest ached. May helped me with closing, then gave me a hand to make sure everything was ready for tomorrow. We worked in silence, side by side. It was nice and comforting to know she was there.

"I don't think I can do this again, May." They were the first words I had spoken in over an hour.

"What can't you do, dear?"

"I can't fall in love again, May, it's too hard."

"Honey, you can't control that, and if you try, you are going to live a life full of regret."

"But I've done this once, look where it got me. I lost him."

"Cass, listen, most people are lucky to find love once in a lifetime. If it is indeed love you feel for Brody, you are one of the blessed ones to have found it twice. Don't throw away a great gift. My Sam passed away when I was only forty, and I vowed I would never let myself fall in love with another man. They came and went, but I stayed true to my word. But there was one fellow, only one I should have never let go. I think of him often and see him often, and every time I do, I wish I had taken that chance and opened myself back up to him."

I wiped my eyes with the back of my hand. "But May, what if he doesn't come back? What if they don't find him?"

She stood for a moment thinking. "Well, if they don't find him, then you will eventually pick yourself back up, dust yourself off like you've done before. You're too young to spend the rest of your life alone. I promise you will be okay. It may not seem like it now, but you will."

"It hurts so much to think about that."

"Then don't, take your thoughts of him not returning, ignore those, and think only thoughts of him returning to you."

"You make it sound so easy, May," I said, placing another handful of books out.

"Dear, I know it's not, but at the same time, it truly is. Christmas is the time for miracles, let's believe in those. Now, I must go, and you should get home and get some rest too, maybe have a talk with Ray. Explain how you feel, you owe him that. Plus, you have a big day tomorrow, and you don't want to look like crap when he comes back, do you?"

I wrapped my arms around her. "Thank you, May."

"Oh, dear, you are very welcome."

I drove up the mountain in silence on my way home. Instead of pulling in my driveway, I drove a little farther and pulled into Ray's driveway. I owed him an explanation of what he had heard today. I shut the engine off and got out of the car. I just prayed I wouldn't be entering in the middle of one of Ray's drunken stupors.

I knocked on the door, the panic that rose in me scared the shit out of even me as I waited for him to answer. It was impossible I would be sick, but my empty stomach still threatened to turn on me. The door finally opened, and Ray looked out at me.

"What?"

"Can I come in?"

"What the hell for, I heard what you said to May."

I looked down at my gloved hands. "I feel like I owe you an explanation."

He glared at me, but eventually, pulled the door open a little further and let me in. He took my coat and led me into the living room, pointing to a spot on the couch.

"Did I make a mistake?" he started.

I bit my bottom lip. I had to tell him the truth of what had happened, and I knew he wasn't going to like it.

"Cass, I love you baby. I need you in my life."

He had never said those words before, and now I knew this was going to be harder than I thought. I closed my eyes.

"I'm sorry you walked in on that conversation with May."

"I'm just praying what I heard you say to May was because he's missing and not because of something else, Cass."

I chewed my bottom lip, trying to figure out how to tell him. When I had garnered up enough courage and went to speak, my words betrayed me and the words that came flying out of my mouth I wished I could have swallowed them back down.

"I slept with him."

"What did you say?" Ray stood up from the chair, clenching his fists together.

"I slept with him, Ray. I didn't mean for it to happen, but it did."

Ray stood there, looking at me with a fierce look of hurt in his eyes.

"We've been in a relationship for two fucking years, it took me over a year to get you in bed, he comes in, and in a week you're in fucking bed with him? Did I mean anything to you at all? What the fuck Cass?" he spat.

I didn't know what to say, but the tears pouring down my cheeks said enough.

"You know, I could tell from the day he showed up at that store, he wanted you and you wanted him. You just didn't see it until I was out of your fucking way. I should have killed his ass that night instead of leaving like you wanted me to." His fists clenched with rage.

"I'm sorry, Ray, please don't hurt me." I couldn't look at him anymore. The truth needed to come out whether he wanted to hear it or not. I couldn't carry it around with me anymore.

"Hope you enjoyed playing house with him while he was here. I don't want you coming back crying to me when he leaves again. We are over."

A deep sob escaped my chest, his words slicing through my heart like a hot knife through butter. I watched through teary eyes as he marched over to the door, throwing my coat and boots out into the snow. He stood with the door open, waiting for me to make my exit, and when I did, he slammed the door shut behind me. I stood outside alone, picking up my coat and slipping my socked feet into my boots.

My chest ached as I walked to my car. I wasn't sure how I made it back to my driveway and don't remember walking into my home. I barely made it to the bathroom —there was no way I could stop the vomit from rising this time.

Chapter Twenty-Nine

CASS

Exhaustion had finally caught up to me. I walked into the little kitchen for a much-needed break and some food. I was completely wiped out, both physically and mentally, but I had to be on my game today. The book drive was in full swing, donations pouring in. Even if people didn't buy anything, it was so nice to see the community coming together. May had been kind enough to send over a couple of her girls to give me a hand when she found out I didn't have any volunteers. Maggie had sent her daughters to lend me a hand as well.

I rested my head against the wall behind me and sipped on a cup of hot coffee. I hadn't slept in days. When

I couldn't take the worry anymore, I had finally broken down and gotten in touch with Brody's boss in the middle of the night to find out they were going to expand the search to the other side of the ski resort. They figured they possibly had gotten turned around and ended up there, there were a few abandoned buildings on that side. This news had calmed me enough to allow me to sleep for a couple of hours.

I poured more hot coffee into my travel mug and grabbed a cookie from the tray I had ordered from the coffee shop for the girls who were helping me. I pulled my cell phone out of my back pocket and went straight to the news. I needed to know if they had found him. The last update from three hours ago said what I already knew. I ate my cookie in silence, reading the words 'ending the search tomorrow if they are not found' repeatedly. Tomorrow was Christmas Eve. I kept reading the article until I heard one of the girls calling from the front.

I sighed, rose from the chair, and stepped out front. Two firefighters stood in full uniform at the counter smiling. One of them was carrying a small box under his arm.

"Cass?"

"Yes."

"It's nice to meet you, I'm Mark, this is Dan." Mark said, nodding toward the other man and holding his hand out to me.

"Nice to meet you."

"Cass, we wanted to stop by. Brody told us all about your book drive and why you are so passionate about what you are doing to help these families. First, we both want to give you our condolences on behalf of the whole department about your husband's passing. Brody told us the story."

"Thank you."

"No, Cass, thank you. You are making such a difference for these families. I want to let you know when Brody first started with us, he set this box out for us to donate. He wanted to be the one to bring this to you today, but under the circumstances, we decided to bring it to you on his behalf."

I couldn't help the lump forming in my throat. They passed me the box, tears forming at the corner of my eyes.

"I... I don't know what to say."

"You don't need to say anything. Your generosity and help to those families shine through. We must be going, it's time for us to get up and start searching that mountain again. We want to bring these guys home. Be strong, we'll find them."

I nodded my head, choking back the tears and sobs I knew were coming. My throat burned, it was so tight, I could barely swallow.

I got both a hot coffee and a couple of cookies before they left. I went back into the kitchen with the box they had brought and set it on the counter, opening it. Inside sat close to a thousand dollars. I couldn't help the tears that started to fall, not because of the amount, but because Brody had done all of this without a single word to me. I was sure, at this moment, I had possibly received my sign.

Chapter Thirty

Cass

Main Street was quiet as I drove home. Big snowflakes had started to fall, and the Christmas displays in the store windows sparkled against the snow. I headed up the hill toward home, grateful things had turned out well for the book drive, but it was hard to be happy without having someone to celebrate with. I turned the radio on and listened to Christmas carols all the way home. I had hoped to catch the news to see if they had been found yet and was disappointed to hear they were still looking.

I drove into the driveway and pulled the car into the garage. Tomorrow was Christmas Eve—if they hadn't found them by then, they were calling off the search, and another Christmas would surely be ruined. My heart was heavy despite all the good I had accomplished today.

I headed inside and was greeted by Missy circling my feet. I filled her now empty bowl and headed to get changed before starting a fire. As soon as that was done, I warmed up a bowl of soup and ate while glued to the news. I grew even more discouraged when they had a live update that they were still searching.

I plugged the tree in, letting the light from it fill the room and curled up on the couch under a warm blanket to watch TV, hoping that being warm would allow me to relax enough to sleep.

As I laid there, my mind constantly ran to the fact time was running out. Another wave of sadness and heaviness came over me. My heart ached, and as much as I could try to deny the fact I didn't want to fall in love, I knew deep down, I was already there. Already there and very much invested and couldn't stand the thought of a possibility I would never get to be held by those arms again or feel his lips against mine. *You've got to come home to me Brody, you can't leave me alone.*

I drifted off, mainly from pure exhaustion once Missy had crawled up on the couch and laid against my chest, the vibration from her purring comforting me enough to fall asleep.

I was awoken by a heavy thudding. I looked around the room, the TV droning in the background, the lights from the tree still softly flashing.

THUD THUD THUD.

Someone was at the front door. Disoriented and half awake, I made my way over to the door. I had no idea what time it was.

THUD THUD THUD.

"Coming," I called out weakly. I pulled the door open to be greeted by two men from the police department.

At the sight of them, I was suddenly very awake, my stomach churning. I swallowed hard, deathly afraid of the news they were going to deliver to me.

"Can, can I help you?"

"Cass Reilly?"

"Yes," I whispered. My eyes starting to burn, the ache in my stomach becoming greater with every passing second.

"We were instructed to stop in and let you know Brody Thompson has been found along with the two other men who were missing up at Prickly Peaks."

I put my hand up to my mouth, the tears starting to pour.

"Are you sure? Is he okay?"

"Yes, miss. Do you want to come with us down to the hospital or do you want to drive yourself?"

I couldn't stop shaking, and suddenly, felt extremely light headed.

"Um, I..."

"Miss, are you alright?" One of the officers stepped forward and grabbed hold of my arm, bracing his other arm around my back as I fell back. He walked inside and took me to the couch where he sat me down.

I heard one of them ask the other to get a glass of water, and soon, I felt a cool cloth pressed to my forehead. I must have been in shock, the room continued spinning out of control.

"Cass, sip some water." I gripped the glass, but I noticed he didn't let it go, instead aiding me to bring the glass to my lips. I sipped the cool water and felt the cool cloth on my head and back of my neck. It took a bit, but after a while, the room stopped spinning, and I started to feel a little better.

"You okay?"

"Hmmm, yes. I feel better now, thank you," I smiled at the officers.

"Now, I think you may want to ride with us down to the hospital. Don't think you should get in the car and drive, miss."

In agreement, I excused myself from the room and ran down the hallway to get changed. I opened the drawer of my dresser to grab a sweatshirt, and that was when I noticed that little wooden box was gone. I glanced around the room to see if maybe I had moved it, but it was nowhere to be found. I thought back, the last time I remembered seeing it was the night I had brought it in here, but I didn't have time to worry about it, I had to get ready and get to Brody.

Locking the front door, I followed the officers to their cruiser. One held the door open for me, and as I was getting in the back seat, a vehicle I didn't recognize pulled into the driveway and stopped just in front of the garage. The front passenger door opened, and someone got out.

It only took the sound of his deep voice calling my name for me to know who it was before I took off across the driveway and crashed into his body. He wrapped his strong arms around me and held me tight. It had never felt so good to be held by someone as it did at that moment.

"You came back," I cried.

"I promised you I would." He kissed me deeply, holding me as if he would never let me go.

Brody

The room dimly lit, we laid in bed, her body pressed to mine, my arms wrapped around her. We hadn't said much to one another. We had shared a tea by the fire in front of the tree, cuddled together on the couch, finally moving to the comfort of her warm soft bed. Something I hadn't had the luxury of sleeping in for a couple of nights.

"I'm so glad you came back to me," I heard her whisper, her fingers tracing small circles in the palm of my hand.

I pressed my lips behind her ear. "I told you I'd be back. That I wasn't going anywhere," I said in a sleepy voice.

I was so comforted by the fact she was lying in my arms, the sound of her slow steady breathing was almost lulling, but I still fought to keep my eyes open in case she needed me. I clasped her hand in mine, kissing her cheek. The tension radiating from her was unsettling. I knew this had been hard on her.

"You can sleep now, baby, I'm here. I'm safe, we're together." I tightened my grip on her, pulling her against me. She rolled her body into me, burying her face into my neck.

"How did you know I haven't slept?" she whispered.

I let out a light chuckle. "Because I didn't sleep, I couldn't. If I gave up for one second thinking about being back here with you, right now, just like this, I don't think I would be here tonight."

"Really?"

"That's how much you mean to me, Cass."

She grew quiet, and I watched as she closed her eyes, comforted by the fact I was there. When her breathing steadied and she relaxed fully in my arms, I too relaxed, comforted by the fact I was in the only place I wanted to be forever, and I fell into a deep restful sleep.

Chapter Thirty-One

We sat together on the floor in front of the fire, the cozy lights from the Christmas tree shining down on us, Christmas music lightly playing in the background. Christmas Eve was here. A half-eaten pizza sat on the floor while we shared the remainder of the bottle of wine we had opened. I sat back against the chair and listened to Brody as he told me the story about what had happened.

"We had been following Tim, he was head of our search team. The wind was blowing the snow so hard, we had almost zero visibility. We took a few more steps forward, and Tim was suddenly gone, he fell down an embankment. We could hear him calling for help, so we slid down to where he was. We figured he had broken his ankle and twisted his knee from the fall. At this point, we were all well passed our rest period, cold, tired, and hungry, but we had no idea where we were, so we had to keep going, we needed to find shelter somewhere. We continued walking from where we had found Tim, he was using us for support, but he was starting to get to the point where he was in so much pain, he wouldn't be able to take much more. We finally came upon an old metal shed-like building. When we got inside, we found five bails of hay which we broke apart and put on the ground, hoping it would insulate us from the cold. I tried to call back to the base to let them know we were alive, but we must have been out of range. I decided to try to call, but my cell phone battery had died from the cold.

"Anyway, we stayed put for the night. Tim was in bad shape, and as soon as he was off his leg, it started to swell. We couldn't leave him there alone, and it was too dangerous for only one of us to try to go back. The wind and snow eventually piled up against the door, basically to the point we couldn't get out the next morning which was good because it served as insulation. I never slept, I couldn't. I couldn't get my mind off you and what you must be going through. I had no idea how long we had been in the shed when I finally heard a voice on the walkie. It was broken up, but it was definitely a voice. We had somehow ended up on an old ski run that had been out of use for a while."

He stopped speaking and took a sip of his wine.

"I was so worried about you. I'm so glad you're okay." I leaned in, kissing him.

"I noticed you did as I asked and didn't snoop," he said, nodding toward the tree, and that was when it dawned on me I hadn't gotten him anything. With all that had gone on over the last week, I had forgotten.

"Brody, I feel horrid, I don't have anything for you."

"That's okay, I don't have anything for you either," he smiled.

"What are you talking about? You told me not to snoop under the tree."

"That's right, but that doesn't mean those are from me," he said smiling.

"Sure, okay, Brody. Whatever you say," I smiled. "Don't try to make me feel better for not getting you anything."

He got up from under the blanket we had been sharing and walked shirtless over to the tree, picking up the two wrapped boxes, and set them in front of me.

"Okay, okay, one of them is from me, you can open that first. The other one I have specific instructions that you open it alone and on Christmas Eve."

I frowned, looking down at the wrapped gifts.

"Open this one first." He sat down, handing me the one package, studying me as I tore at the paper.

I opened the taped box, pulled away the red tissue paper inside, and there in my hands sat the same frame Ray had broken, only this one was brand new, and it contained the exact same picture of Jackson and me. I didn't know what to say.

"How did you do this?"

"Well, I was the one who originally picked up the frame Jackson had ordered, so I knew where to get it. And you don't remember, but I was the one who took that picture the summer I visited you guys. I dug through a couple of boxes of mine and found the card it was on. I couldn't stand to see you so upset that night. I went and replaced it the next day. I knew how much it meant to you."

"Thank you, Brody." A lone tear fell onto my hand as I stared at the picture. "I don't know what to say."

"You don't need to say anything." He leaned down and pulled my chin up and kissed me softly. "Now, I'm going to head down to the bedroom and leave you alone to open the other one."

I looked up at him. "What is it?"

"I don't know, open it and find out." He kissed my cheek and went toward the bedroom.

I sat with the wrapped gift in front of me. There was no card, or tag, I had no idea who it was from or what could be in the box. When I finally built up the courage to open it, I gently tore the paper. Inside sat the little locked wooden box with my name engraved on it. I frowned and pulled on the little lock just like I had done when I found the box, but it still wouldn't open. I was just about to yell to Brody when I flipped over the box and found a little key taped to the bottom. I had checked that, there had been no key before. I took the key and inserted it into the bottom of the little lock and turned it, hearing a little click, and the lock sprung open.

Inside sat a single envelope with my name on it. My hands started to shake as I picked up the envelope. I recognized the handwriting right away. I took a deep breath, the pit of my stomach rising into my chest, making me feel uneasy.

I pulled out the folded piece of paper, carefully unfolding it, staring down at Jackson's handwriting. I wiped away the tears that had clouded my vision, took a drink of my wine, and began to read.

My dearest Cass,

I'm glad this letter found its way to you, then again, I'm not. If you are reading it, it must mean I have passed, otherwise, you would never have been given this box. Cass, my love, my life, I hope I gave you everything you ever dreamed of while we were together. I hope never a day went by that I disappointed you or let you down. To me, you were perfect, my everything. I hope you know I loved you with all my heart.

I want to give you something, Cass, a last Christmas gift if you will. Perhaps you are still just as lost as the day I passed away. It's okay if you are, it will pass. What I want to give you is a confirmation that you are doing things right, I want to give you permission to start over. Regardless of where you are, let me give you this, Cass. Live your life, baby. Don't dwell on the fact I am not here anymore as I am always with you and will be with you, always. No matter what, I will be watching from above to see all your accomplishments, and I'll be beside you to help calm your fears until the next person comes to take my place.

Whatever you do, don't give up on your dreams. Please, don't ever let anyone take those away from you.

If the man who is going to take my place has already arrived or you are unsure about who he may be, listen to me. Love without abandon, be with someone who makes your soul hum, who can make you smile just by looking at you, who can turn you on just by touching you. Be with someone who takes the time to listen to every problem you have, no matter how small it is. If it matters to you, it should to them. Be with someone who understands the troubles you go through when you write because you are talented, Cass, I never told you that enough. Make sure he will help you work out plot troubles, comfort you when you kill a character, and he's okay with it when you burn dinner because you are on a deadline. Lord knows, I ate lots of burned dinners.

Don't just settle, you deserve the world, Cass. The world I wish I could have given you. But since I can't, I promise you this. If you follow those steps, you will be given the world. I'm sorry I couldn't be the one to give it to you, and I guess that is how I have let you down.

I flipped the letter over in my hand. That was it, that was all that there was. I could barely breathe as I dropped the letter into my lap, sobs shaking my whole body. There was no question in my mind who I needed to be with, I already knew, and Jackson had just confirmed it, he had answered my prayers.

I sat for a while, reading and rereading the letter before heading down the hall to find Brody. He was in his room, sitting on the edge of his bed, his back to the door. I leaned against the door frame, watching him for a few minutes. He didn't even know I was there or at least, I thought he didn't until he spoke.

"He was always planning, Cass, always. When we were alone, he was constantly worried about what would happen to you if anything should happen to him. It was like he had some freakish way of knowing he wasn't going to be around long."

"You took that box from my dresser?"

"Yep. He told me what the box looked like and had given me the key. I had looked for it numerous times after he had passed away but could never find it. When I saw it that day you found it, I made sure to grab it and hide it when you were in the shower one morning. His instructions to me had been clear... *When she meets someone, I want you to give it to her. The first Christmas they are together.*"

"Is that really why you came back, Brody, to give me the box?"

"Why would that be, Cass, I didn't have the box? I came back here for one last chance with you. But when you found the box, I figured you deserved to have whatever he left for you, Cass. It was important to him, he wanted you to have it, and I figured since I have fucked up so much and let him down enough over the last couple of years, this was my chance at redemption with him."

"Do you even know what was in the box, Brody?"

"Not a fucking clue, Cass."

I stepped forward, but Brody refused to look at me. I held out the letter to him.

"Read it."

He kept his head down, his rough fingers grazing my hand, sending a jolt right to my center as he took the paper from me and opened it.

"In that letter, he has described someone who is very special to me. Someone who I can see myself spending the rest of my life with."

Brody sat silently, still not meeting my eyes. "No worries, Cass, I'll pack up and be on my way, so you can be with him."

"Ray is gone, Brody. It's over. Honestly, it has been over since the day you walked into my store. I don't think it was ever meant to happen with him."

"It's over? So, he's gone?"

"Yes. You're the one. You make me feel all those things in the letter. You are the one I am supposed to be with, Brody. Truthfully, I think you're the one he wanted me to be with."

I walked closer to him, taking the letter from his hand and pushed my way in between his legs. I sat the letter on the bed beside him, took hold of both of his hands, wrapping them around my waist. It was only a matter of moments before I felt his hands grip into my ass to pull me closer to him.

"I meant what I said, I couldn't wait for you to come

home. This is your home now. I'm in love with you, Brody, I don't think I ever stopped. My anger just sidetracked my feelings for you."

"I'm in love with you too." He lifted my shirt and pressed a soft kiss to my stomach.

Chapter Thirty-Two

Cass

I was cleaning up the store and removing the tables and the remainder of books from the book drive after locking up for the night. Brody had gone out of town with a couple of the guys from the fire department and wouldn't be back until later tonight. I had just received my shipment of new releases late in the afternoon and needed to get them out on the shelves for tomorrow, the start of my boxing week and New Years' sale.

I had just put away the two folding tables that had occupied floor space and packed away the three remaining shelves of donations, loading them into the back of my car to take to the library. Walking back into the store room, I loaded up my little cart with some boxes of my new shipment and headed back out front.

A light tapping on the front window caused me to pause while placing the books on the shelf above my head. I turned to see who it was and was shocked to find Ray standing with his face pressed up to the glass. We hadn't spoken since the night he threw me out.

He signaled to the front door to let him in. I was hesitant. He had never hurt me physically, but as angry as he had been that night, I wasn't sure letting him in while I was alone was the best idea. I pointed to the closed sign and shrugged my shoulders. I watched as he took his phone out of his pocket and typed out something. My phone vibrated in my pocket. Pulling out my phone I looked at the message.

Ray: I just want to talk.

I looked at Ray, not knowing what I should do. Brody had suggested I stay far away from him. My phone vibrated again in my hand.

Ray: Please, just talk, no anger

I sighed, looking at all the work I needed to get done, then back to the window, his sad eyes pleading with me. I walked over to the door and let him in.

"Hey."

"Hey," I replied.

"How have you been?"

"I'm fine," I answered curtly, walking back over to where I was working.

Ray watched me as I emptied another box, moving onto the next one.

"I miss you, Cass," he said quietly. I closed my eyes, holding onto the books in my hand. "I miss us."

I didn't say anything, I couldn't. Of course, I missed him and the time we had spent together, but my heart belonged to another. It had all along, it had just taken me a while to figure it out.

"I want to apologize for the way I behaved the other night. You were just being honest with me, but it crushed me that you would do that to me, but I realize things happen. I shouldn't have acted the way I did."

"Well, it's done." I had nothing else to say to that and continued organizing the shelves.

"Cass, I want to be with you. I want us."

As I continued to carry on with what I was doing, I finally felt his warm hands on my arm. His touch had provided comfort for me for three years, but now it did nothing.

"Please, baby, I forgive you. I want us."

I shook my head no but stayed silent.

"Please, Cass. I love you."

Brody

I walked quietly through the back door of the bookstore. I was here early and was surprised to find Cass still at work, so I decided to surprise her. I knew she had wanted to get a lot done tonight. I quietly closed the door behind me and walked up to the front of the building. As soon as I saw what was going on out in the front room, I stopped dead in the doorway. Ray stood, his hands on her shoulders.

"Cass, I love you." His voice sounded restrained and sad.

I watched, not saying a word, my heart in my throat, the silence between the two of them so loud.

"Please, Cass, I need you to come back to me," he whispered, running his hands over her shoulders.

My first instinct was to charge in there and drop him, but I stood completely frozen to my spot. Why wasn't she saying anything?

I had to turn away, I couldn't watch this anymore. I couldn't bear to see what was going to happen between the two of them. I was just about to give up and leave when I heard her tiny voice answer.

"Ray, we're over. Everything that has happened over the last two months with Brody coming back has shown me I'm in love with him, Ray. I'm in love with Brody, and I always have been. My heart belongs to him."

"Well, I guess that's all I need to hear. Goodbye, Cass."

Tears stung my eyes. She hadn't really told me that. Sure, we had exchanged I love yous, but she hadn't said it like that.

I watched Ray, without another word, his head hung low, leave through the front door, leaving Cass to stand there alone. He stopped outside the store window for a moment and placed his hand on the glass, looking at her, almost like he was taking a mental picture of the way she looked before he walked away for good. After he was gone, I watched her walk over and lock the door.

"Goodbye," she mumbled.

I didn't want her to know I had heard what was going on, so I quietly slipped back to the back of the building and opened and closed the back door, shutting it hard enough so she would hear it.

"Hello?" She called.

"It's just me, Cass," I called as I walked out to the front. She was in the same spot, loading books up onto the shelf as if nothing had happened.

"I thought you wouldn't be back until later tonight?"

"That was the plan, but we decided to come back

earlier. I saw you were still here, so I thought I would stop."

"Great! Maybe an early night then," she winked and smiled, looking over her shoulder in my direction.

I came up behind her and took the books from her hand, putting them down on the cart and pulled her into my arms.

"Distracting me already."

She smiled up at me as I looked into her eyes. "I love you." I placed my hand on her cheek, leaned in, and kissed her.

"I love you too, Brody," she whispered when we parted.

"What do you say we head home?"

"I'd like that." Pressing her lips against mine, I knew I had finally found my way home.

Chapter Thirty-Three

"Half hour until midnight!" I called out the back door while holding onto Missy. Brody came through the sliding door, carrying the last bucket of wood he planned on bringing in for the night. Snow had been dumping heavily most of the day which caused me to have to shut the store early and come home. "Do you think that's enough wood?" I asked, closing the door behind him.

"It should last us a few days, long enough until I can at least clean out a path to the woodpile once the storm stops." I locked the back door and pulled the heavy curtains across the cold glass, shutting out the raging storm.

"Did you want another tea? Or a hot chocolate?"

"Hot chocolate." He looked over his shoulder at me and smiled as he took his coat off and started unloading the wood from the basket onto the large pile. "With whipped cream," he called.

While waiting for the milk to warm, I stood back and watched Brody carefully stacking the wood, then throw a few pieces into the fire. Finally, for the first time in a long time, I could say I was happy, content, and that the house felt like home.

I poured the warm milk into the mugs, dumping generous amounts of chocolate into each cup and stirring them, then spraying them both with a dollop of whipped cream. I carried both mugs into the living room and headed back over to the couch where we had been curled up together while I wrote, and Brody watched TV. I sat back down and pulled the laptop onto my lap. I only had another half a chapter to write before I hit the end of the short story. Brody settled onto the couch beside me.

I had been typing away for about fifteen mins when Brody rested his chin on my shoulder to read what I was writing.

"What you working on? Anything fun that maybe we can work through together?" He winked as I met his eyes.

"Maybe," I giggled and turned my attention back to the screen.

"You almost finished for tonight?

"Maybe ten more minutes or so," I said, deep in thought, trying to get this idea down before it escaped me.

"I really want some attention baby," he said, putting his arm around me.

I did my best to ignore his pouting lips, but when he grabbed my hand, pulled it away from the keyboard, and placed it on his hard, throbbing cock, it was much harder to ignore. I turned to face him, his lips meeting mine with need and hunger, his tongue sweeping deep into my mouth. He lifted the laptop from my lap and put it on the table, crashing back into me before I could protest, running his hands over my body.

"Brody, please, I really need to get this finished," I said giggling, reaching for the laptop, but Brody pushed me back against the couch.

"Nope, you're mine! I plan to be inside of you at the start of the new year."

Brody got up from the couch, effortlessly picked me up from where I was sitting, and carried me into the bedroom. I let out a loud laugh as he threw me on the bed and pulled my pants from my body. Sliding the bottom of my shirt up, he trailed kisses down my abdomen, his fingers tracing the edge of the waistband of my panties.

"I want to rip these babies off of you," he growled.

"No way, they're my favorite." I let out a little giggle and raised my butt a little, so I could slide them off.

He knelt on the bed, kissing me. I pulled at the back of

his shirt and it quickly found its way to the floor, along with his lounge pants. Crawling between my legs, he allowed me to lock mine around his waist. I watched as he stroked himself a couple of times before he placed himself at my entrance and slid into me.

We lay under the covers together, our sweaty bodies wrapped up in one another, Missy curled up at our feet.

"God, I love making love to you." Brody whispered into my ear, breathless. He placed gentle kisses along my neck, just below my ear, and pulled me against him.

I glanced at the time, just a little after one.

"We missed the new year," I giggled.

"No, we didn't, I was right where I said I would be, and you were right where I wanted you, moaning my name," he quietly whispered in my ear.

I rolled into his chest, his arms wrapping around my body as I buried my face into his neck, breathing in his scent. He was right, I was right where I wanted to be, wrapped in the comfort of his arms on this silent night.

Epilogue

Cass - Two Years Later

I glanced down at my watch, it was a little after one. I figured Brody would be here soon as I placed the last book that was in the box on the shelf. My back was killing me. I was so done with being pregnant. Jessica was helping a couple customers out front, so I was going to head to the back and have a break when I heard the front bell jingle.

"Cass, there you are." May came strolling in the store, carrying her bag of knitting. "I have something for you, dear." She plopped the bag on the counter and pulled out a beautifully knit afghan in an array of colors.

"May, this is beautiful. Thank you."

"I can't stay and chat, dear, but I wanted to drop this

off to you while you were still here. That little bundle will be arriving any day now," she said resting her hand on my belly. As if in response to her, the baby gave a pretty good kick. May let out a laugh.

"I was just going to go have some tea, do you want to join me, May?"

"I can't, dear. I have a date with my ladies for a knitting class. You should give it a try again."

I let out a small giggle. "I'll stick to my writing."

"Alright, dear, it's never too late to change your mind." She waved and headed out the door. I looked down at the blanket in my hands and smiled to myself.

"You okay out here, Jessica?"

"Of course, go on and take a rest."

"Would you like some tea?" I asked.

"Yes, please."

I waddled into the back room, put the kettle on, and sat down at the table.

"Cass!" I heard the back door open and Brody's deep voice call my name.

"In here."

Brody came strolling into the shop, carrying a small box.

"Hey gorgeous." He sat the box on the table and leaned down and gave me a kiss, placing his hand on my belly. "How are you feeling?"

"Tired. I'm ready to be done with this. Whatever you

do, don't get me pregnant again, okay?" I smiled, kissing him again. "What's in the box?"

"Why don't you open it, it's for you."

Brody pulled his pocket knife out and cut through the tape, sliding the box over to me. I opened the flaps, and inside sat a few paperback copies of my newest release from my publisher with a simple note. I picked up the piece of paper and read it aloud. "Cass, congrats on hitting the top ten!" Tears flooded my eyes.

"Congrats, babe, she called just as I got home. I knew you would want me to bring this down."

"I owe it all to you," I said, taking his hand in mine.

"Nope, you're the one with the talent."

I heard Jessica call my name from out front. "Coming," I called.

Brody took my hand and helped me up from where I was sitting and followed me out front, carrying the small box of books. Ray stood on the other side of the counter.

"Ray," I smiled, "how are things?"

"Good, Cass. How are you?"

"I'm doing well. Thanks."

Out of the corner of my eye, I saw Brody hand Jessica the small box of books and watched as she went over and placed them on the shelf that held all my other republished titles. He came up behind me and wrapped his arm around my waist.

"Ray," he nodded.

I hadn't seen Ray since the night he had been at the store. He had written me a letter explaining he had retired from working on vehicles at his garage and was taking on more of a managerial role, scheduling and looking after the books. Once that transition had taken over, Ray sold his house and decided to move down south for a while with a couple of his friends. I had heard recently he was back in town and living in a condo just off the water.

"Brody. I ran into May earlier today. I wanted to come by and congratulate you both." He handed me a bag, a yellow teddy bear peaking up over the edge of the bag.

"Thank you." I gave him a gentle smile.

I walked around the counter and gave him a hug. I didn't hold any bad feelings toward him anymore. Brody and I had talked about the whole situation. I had decided that if Ray was back for good, Brody needed to know it was important to me to have Ray in my life in some way.

"Don't be a stranger, okay? We want to have you over for a barbeque after the baby is born," I whispered.

"That sounds good, Cass, I'd like that."

He let me go and looked to Brody. "Make sure you take care of her."

"Always, Ray." Brody held out his hand to Ray. They shook hands for the first time, and Ray headed back toward the door.

I watched as he walked outside and back down the

street. Brody came up behind me, placing his hands on my shoulders.

"What do you say we head home for the night?"

I nodded, grabbing his hand with mine. "Jessica, you okay to lock up tonight?"

"Of course, Mrs. Thompson. I'm good."

I grabbed my purse from the back room and hand in hand, we walked out to Brody's truck and headed home to celebrate.

Connor Jackson was born just shy of midnight a couple of weeks later with Brody at my side, coaching me every step of the way. Together, as we looked down into that innocent little face, nothing had ever felt more complete.

A Note from the Author

Dear Readers,

I would like to thank you for taking the time to read On A Silent Night. Christmas has always been a special time of year for me, and somehow it is always filled with magic no matter what I am going through.

I hope you enjoyed Cass and Brody's story. If you did, I would love it if you would drop me a review. Reviews are important to me, I love to hear what my readers thought.

Back to You this Christmas

Alexa – Earlier that year

While I sat waiting for the plane to board, I sipped on my coffee and fiddled with my phone. The airport was busy, as always, and I was on my way to my next photo shoot location. I had spent the last three years freelancing as a photographer and had traveled halfway around the world, visiting places like Paris, Italy, France, and Australia. It had been a wonderful experience, and at the young age of twenty-six, I had seen more of the world than people double my age. The traveling was amazing and part of the reason why I had gone into this line of work, but lately it wasn't enough; I felt something important was missing.

Those feelings began two days ago, while I was photographing this girl, Jasmine, on the day of her wedding with her mother. As I looked at them, laughing, through the lens of my camera, I began to miss home something terrible. Not only did I miss my parents, but I missed my bed, the sounds of the house, the homemade meals, everything. I had to put those feeling out of my mind in order to go on with rest of my day, being as happy and professional as I could, even though I was fighting back tears.

When I'd returned to my apartment that night, I was exhausted. I'd dropped my equipment to the floor and headed into the kitchen to make tea. However, it wasn't long before I found myself curled up on the kitchen floor crying my eyes out over everything that had happened over the last year. I'd hit a rough patch, and something had to change.

Eight months earlier, I had started dating my boss, something I had sworn I would never do, but he had been charming and relentless, so I had given in. Things had been going well, almost too well, and then what I feared the most happened. I had returned to the office after a rather rough day four weeks ago, and I'd found a letter addressed to me sitting on my desk. It was late, I was tired, so I shoved the envelope in my bag planning to read it at home. That had been a good plan on my part because inside the envelope, I'd found a letter explaining that things weren't working out between us and he thought it would better if we parted ways. We were over and I'd been fired.

For whatever reason, I hadn't been able to get the letter out of my mind. I'd wiped the tears from my cheek and blew my nose. I'd desperately needed to talk to my mother, so I'd pulled my phone from my pocket and dialed home. I'd needed to hear her voice and crossed my fingers that she was home, and she answered. I'd felt so defeated and wondered if maybe it was time I went home for a longer visit than my regular thirty-six-hour period.

Mom's voice finally broke through the other end of the phone. "Hey, sweetie, you're calling late." Then her voice quivered a little. "Everything okay?"

Shit, I had forgotten to do the time conversion before I called. It had to be eleven at night back at home.

"Everything is fine, Mom. Just really missing home," I answered quickly, sniffling and picking at my broken fingernail. I didn't blame her for worrying. I was her baby, off on the other side of the world, most of the time in the middle of nowhere, generally photographing animals and local people for magazine articles. Of course, she would worry when I made a call this late at night.

"Lexi you don't sound okay."

"Just a tough day, I guess. What's new?" I wanted to change the subject. I didn't want to focus on the troubles I'd had today. Hell, I still hadn't told her that I had broken up with Gary and that I'd been fired. I'd been holding out because I didn't want her to worry about me. She still didn't even know that I was working for someone else.

"Well, really, we are just getting ready for the wedding tomorrow."

"What wedding?" I asked, sniffling.

"Drew and Laura's. Your brother just got in tonight and they've gone out celebrating. I wish you could be here for this. I know Drew would have loved to have you there."

"Wow, really, already?" I glanced up to the calendar that hung on the wall and, sure enough, the large red heart I had drawn around the date stood out to me. I had received an invitation in the mail, but my bank account had ultimately decided for me that I couldn't go. I figured they would understand why I couldn't make it, and knowing Drew, he had probably sent me the invitation out of courtesy. He'd probably expected me not to be there. "I couldn't afford it, Mom."

"You should have said something. We would have paid for you to come home. We miss you, Lex."

"I know, Mom. I miss you guys too." I sniffled again. I got up off the floor and took a sip of my tea and pulled something to eat out of the fridge while listening to Mom talk about one of the neighbors. I took my plate of cheese and crackers over to the small table and sat down, picking up a pencil to write something down quickly.

"Oh, and your brother is coming home for Christmas

this year," she said, changing the subject once again. "Would be nice if you could join us."

I fiddled with the pencil, holding back tears. I would give anything to sleep in my own bed, breathing in the familiar scent of Downy scented sheets. Right about now, I wanted nothing more than to taste one of her home-cooked meals and fresh-baked goodies too. I could barely cook, and I certainly couldn't bake. I stared down at my half-eaten cheese and crackers and pushed the food around on my plate while thinking about how close to heaven her food would be right about now.

"I know, Mom. Maybe next year."

We talked for another twenty minutes before I had to get off the phone with her. If I hadn't, I was sure the tears would start to fall as we talked about old times. I choked down my meal in silence, just like I had done most nights since I had been gone. When I put my dirty plate back in the kitchen, I turned and looked up at the calendar, that bright-red heart screaming at me. I let out a deep breath. She was so lucky to have him, I thought to myself and picked up the invitation that sat on the pile of mail on the table. These had to have been expensive, I thought to myself as I ran my fingers over the gold-leaf paper. Laura was so lucky. I threw the invitation down, took a couple of cookies from the bag on the counter, and my tea, and headed into the other room to watch some TV.

Fifty minutes later, the thought of home still hadn't

left my mind, and I had begun checking out every airline for a flight home, finally booking one for December. I put it on my credit card, since my bank account certainly couldn't handle the cost of a flight right now, and decided that I would worry about it later.

As I sat waiting for the boarding call for my flight, I counted the weeks until I would be home—only twenty-six more weeks. I was so excited. This Christmas I would be sitting around the tree with my family for two weeks, instead of wallowing alone in misery.

Read Back to You this Christmas Today!